Croatian Tales of Long Ago

The Myths, Legends and Folk Stories of Croatia

By Ivana Brlić-Mažuranić

Translated by F. S. Copeland

Illustrations by Vladimir Kirin

PANTIANOS
CLASSICS

Published by Pantianos Classics

ISBN-13: 978-1-78987-275-0

First published in 1916

This edition is adapted from the English translation of 1922

Contents

How Quest Sought the Truth 6

    II 10

    III 12

    IV 15

    V 17

    VI 18

    VII 23

Fisherman Plunk and His Wife 24

    II 32

    III 36

Reygoch 39

    II 46

Bridesman Sun and Bride Bridekins 55

Stribor's Forest 64

    II 66

    III 69

Little Brother Primrose and Sister Lavender 74

    II 75

    III 76

    IV 78

    V 79

VI 81

VII 82

VIII 84

IX 85

X 87

XI 88

XII 89

XIII 91

XIV 95

XV 96

XVI 97

XVII 98

XVIII 99

XIX 100

Notes 102

Interpretation of Names, etc. 102

How Quest Sought the Truth

ONCE upon a time very long ago there lived an old man in a glade in the midst of an ancient forest. His name was Witting, and he lived there with his three grandsons. Now this old man was all alone in the world save for these three grandsons, and he had been father and mother to them from the time when they were quite little. But now they were full-grown lads, so tall that they came up to their grandfather's shoulder, and even taller. Their names were Bluster, Careful and Quest.

One spring morning old Witting got up early, before the sun had risen, called his three grandsons and told them to go into the wood where they had gathered honey last year; to see how the little bees had come through the winter, and whether they had waked up yet from their winter sleep. Careful, Bluster and Quest got up, dressed, and went out.

It was a good way to the place where the bees lived. Now all three brothers knew every pathway in the woods, and so they strode cheerily and boldly along through the great forest. All the same it was somewhat dark and eerie under the trees, for the sun was not yet up and neither bird nor beast stirring. Presently the lads began to feel a little scared in that great silence, because just at dawn, before sunrise, the wicked Rampogusto, King of Forest Goblins, loves to range the forest, gliding softly from tree to tree in the gloom.

So the brothers started to ask one another about all the wonderful things there might be in the world. But as not one of them had ever been outside the forest, none could tell the others anything about the world; and so they only became more and more depressed. At last, to keep up their courage a bit, they began to sing and call upon All-Rosy to bring out the Sun:

> Little lord All-Rosy bright.
> Bring golden Sun to give us light;
> Show thyself, All-Rosy bright,
> Loora-la, Loora-la lay!

Singing at the top of their voices, the lads walked through the woods towards a spot from where they could see a second range of mountains. As they neared the spot they saw a light above those mountains brighter than they had ever seen before, and it fluttered like a golden banner.

The lads were dumbfounded with amazement, when all of a sudden the light vanished from off the mountain and reappeared above a great rock nearer at hand, then still nearer, above an old limetree, and at last shone like burnished gold right in front of them. And then they saw that it was a lovely youth in glittering raiment, and that it was his golden cloak which fluttered like a golden banner. They could not bear to look upon the face of the youth, but covered their eyes with their hands for very fear.

"Why do you call me, if you are afraid of me, you silly fellows?" laughed the golden youth—for he was All-Rosy. "You call on All-Rosy, and then you are afraid of All-Rosy. You talk about the wide world, but you do not know the wide world. Come along with me and I will show you the world, both earth and heaven, and tell you what is in store for you."

Thus spoke All-Rosy, and twirled his golden cloak so that he caught up Bluster, Careful and Quest, all three in its shimmering folds. Round went All-Rosy and round went the cloak, and the brothers, clinging to the hem of the cloak, spun round with it, round and round and round again, and all the world passed before their eyes. First they saw all the treasure and all the lands and all the possessions and the riches that were then in the world. And they went on whirling round and round and round again, and saw all the armies, and all spears and all arrows and all the captains and all plunder which were then in the world. And the cloak twirled yet more quickly, round and round and round again, and all of a sudden they saw all the stars, great and small, and the moon and the Seven Sisters and the winds and all the clouds. The brothers were quite dazed with so many sights, and still the cloak went on twirling and whirling with a rustling, rushing sound like a golden banner. At last the golden hem fluttered down; and Bluster, Careful and Quest stood once more on the turf. Before them stood the golden youth All-Rosy as before, and said to them:

"There, my lads, now you have seen all there is to see in the world. Listen to what is in store for you and what you must do to be lucky."

At that the brothers became more scared than ever, yet they pricked up their ears and paid good heed, so as to remember everything very carefully. But All-Rosy went on at once:

"There! this is what you must do. Stay in the glade, and don't leave your grandfather until he leaves you; and do not go into the world, neither for good nor for evil, until you have repaid your grandfather for all his love to you." And as All-Rosy said this, he twirled his cloak round and vanished, as though he had never been; and lo, it was day in the forest.

But Rampogusto, King of the Forest Goblins, had seen and heard everything. Like a wraith of mist he had slipped from tree to tree and kept himself hidden from the brothers among the branches of an old beech-tree.

7

Rampogusto had always hated old Witting. He hated him as a mean scoundrel hates an upright man, and above all things he hated him because the old man had brought the sacred fire to the glade so that it might never go out, and the smoke of that fire made Rampogusto cough most horribly.

So Rampogusto wasn't pleased with the idea that the brothers should obey All-Rosy, and stay beside their grandfather and look after him; but he bethought himself how he could harm old Witting, and somehow turn his grandsons against him.

Therefore, no sooner had Bluster, Careful and Quest recovered from their amazement and turned to go home than Rampogusto slipped swiftly, like a cloud before the wind, to a wooded glen where there was a big osier clump, which was chock-full of goblins—tiny, ugly, humpy, grubby, boss-eyed, and what not, all playing about like mad creatures. They squeaked and they squawked, they jumped and they romped; they were a pack of harum-scarum imps, no good to anybody and no harm either, so long as a man did not take them into his company. But Rampogusto knew how to manage that.

So he picked out three of them, and told them to jump each on one of the brothers, and see how they might harm old Witting through his grandsons.

Now while Rampogusto was busy choosing his goblins, Bluster, Careful and Quest went on their way; and so scared were they that they clean forgot all they had seen during their flight and everything that All-Rosy had told them.

So they came back to the cabin, and sat down on a stone outside and told their grandfather what had happened to them.

"And what did you see as you were flying round, and what did All-Rosy tell you?" Witting asked Careful, his eldest grandson. Now Careful was in a real fix, because he had clean forgotten, neither could he remember what All-Rosy had told him. But from under the stone where they were sitting crept a wee hobgoblin—ugly and horned and grey as a mouse.

The goblin tweaked Careful's shirt from behind and whispered: "Say: I have seen great riches, hundreds of beehives, a house of carved wood and heaps of fine furs. And All-Rosy said to me: 'Thou shalt be the richest of all the three brothers.'"

Careful never bothered to think whether this was the truth that the imp was suggesting, but just turned and repeated it word for word to his grandfather. No sooner had he spoken than the goblin hopped into his pouch, curled himself up in a corner of the pouch—and there stopped!

Then Witting asked Bluster, the second grandson, what he might have seen in his flight, and what All-Rosy might have told him? And Bluster, too, had noticed nothing and remembered nothing. But from under the stone crept the second hobgoblin, quite small, ill-favoured, horned and smutty as a pole-cat. The goblin plucked Bluster by the shirt and whispered: "Say: I saw lots of armed men, many bows and arrows and slaves galore in chains. And All-Rosy said to me: 'Thou shalt be the mightiest of the brothers.'"

Bluster considered no more than Careful had done, but was very pleased, and lied to his grandfather even as the goblin had prompted him. And the goblin at once jumped on his neck and crawled down his shirt, hid in his bosom, and stopped there.

Now the grandfather asked the youngest grandson, Quest, but he, too, could recall nothing. And from under the stone crept the third hobgoblin, the youngest, the ugliest, horned with big horns, and black as a mole.

The hobgoblin tugged Quest by the shirt and whispered: "Say: I have seen all the heavens and all the stars and all clouds. And All-Rosy said to me:

'Thou shalt be the wisest among men and know what the winds say and the stars tell.'"

But Quest loved the truth, and so he would not listen to the goblin nor lie to his grandfather, but kicked the goblin and said to his grandfather:

"I don't know, grandfather, what I saw or what I heard."

The goblin gave a squeal, bit Quest's foot, and then scuttled away under the stone like a lizard. But Quest gathered potent herbs and bound up his foot with them, so that it might heal quickly.

II

Now the goblin whom Quest had kicked first scooted away under the stone, and then wriggled into the grass, and hopped off through the grass into the woods, and through the woods into the osier clump.

He went up to Rampogusto all shaking with fright and said: "Rampogusto, dread sovereign, I wasn't able to jump on that youth whom you gave into my care."

Then Rampogusto fell into a frightful rage, because he knew those three brothers well, and most of all he feared Quest, lest he should remember the truth. For if Quest were to remember the truth, why, then Rampogusto would never be able to get rid of old Witting nor the sacred fire.

So he seized the little goblin by the horns, picked him up and dusted him soundly with a big birchrod.

"Go back!" he roared—"go back to the young man, and it will be a black day for you if ever he remembers the truth!"

With these words Rampogusto let the goblin go; and the goblin, scared half out of his wits, squatted for three days in the osier clump and considered and considered how he might fulfil his difficult task. "I shall have as much trouble with Quest, for sure, as Quest with me," reflected the goblin. For he was a scatter-brained little silly, and did not care at all for a tiresome job.

But while he squatted in the osier clump those other two imps were already at work, the one in Careful's pouch and the other in Bluster's bosom. From that day forth Careful and Bluster began to rove over hill and dale, and even slept but little at home—and all because of the goblins!

There was the goblin curled up in the bottom of Careful's pouch, and that goblin loved riches better than the horn over his right eye.

So all day long he butted Careful in the ribs, teasing and goading him on: "Hurry up, get on! We must seek, we must find! Let's look for bees, let's gather honey, and then we will keep a tally with rows and rows of scores!"

So said the goblin, because in those days they reckoned up a man's possessions with tallies.

Now a tally is only a long wooden stick with a notch cut in it for every sum that is owing to a man!

But Bluster's goblin butted him in the breast, and that goblin wanted to be the strongest of all and lord of all the earth. So he worried and worried Bluster, and urged him to roam through the woods looking for young ash plants and slender maple saplings to make a warrior's outfit and weapons. "Hurry up, get on!" teased the goblin. "You must seek, you must find! Spears, bows and arrows to suit a hero's mind, so that man and beast may tremble before us."

And both Bluster and Careful listened to their goblins, and went off after their own concerns as the goblins led them.

But Quest stayed with his grandfather that day and yet other three days, and all the time he puzzled and puzzled over whatever it was that All-Rosy might have told him; because Quest wanted to tell his grandfather the truth; but, alas! he could not remember it at all!

So that day went by, and the next, and so three days; and on the third day Quest said to his grandfather:

"Good-bye, grandfather. I am going to the hills, and shall not come back until I remember the truth, if it should take me ten years."

Now Witting's hair was grey, and there was little he cared for in this world except his grandson Quest, and him he loved and cherished as a withered leaf cherishes a drop of dew. So the old man started sadly and said:

"What good will the truth be to me, my boy, when I may be dead and gone long before you remember it?"

This he said, and in his heart he grieved far more even than he showed in his words; and he thought: "How could the boy leave me!"

But Quest replied:

"I must go, grandfather, because I have thought it out, and that seems the right thing to me."

Witting was a wise old man, and considered: "Perhaps there is more wisdom in a young head than in an old one; only if the poor lad is doing wrong it's a sad weird he will have to dree—because he is so gentle and upright." And as Witting thought of that he grew sadder than ever, but said nothing more. He just kissed his grandson good-bye and bade him go where he wished.

But Quest's heart sadly misgave him because of his grandfather, and he very, very nearly changed his mind on the threshold and stayed beside him. But he forced himself to do as he had made up his mind to, and went out and away into the hills.

Just as Quest parted from his grandfather his imp thought he might as well get out of the osier clump and tackle that tiresome job; and he reached the clearing just as Quest was hurrying away.

So Quest went off to the hills, very downcast and sad; and when he came to the first rock, lo and behold, there was the goblin, gibbering.

"Why," thought Quest, "it's the very same one—quite small, misshapen, black as a mole and with big horns."

11

The goblin stood right in Quest's way, and would not let him pass. So Quest got angry with the little monster for hindering him like this; he picked up a stone, threw it at the goblin, and hit him squarely between the horns. "Now I've killed him," thought Quest.

But when he looked again there was the goblin as spry as ever, and two more horns had sprouted where the stone had hit him!

"Well, evidently stones won't drive him off," said Quest. So he went round the goblin and forward on his way. But the imp scuttled on in front of him, to the right and to the left, and then straight in front, for all the world like a rabbit.

At last they came to a little level spot between cliffs—a very stony place; and on one side of it there was a deep well-spring. "Here will I stay," said Quest; and he at once spread out his sheep-skin coat under a crab-tree and sat down, so that he might reflect in peace and remember what All-Rosy had verily and truly told him.

But when the imp saw that, he squatted down straight in front of Quest under the tree, played silly tricks on him, and worried him horribly. He chased lizards under Quest's feet, threw burrs at his shirt, and slipped grass-hoppers up his sleeves.

"Oh dear, this is most annoying!" thought Quest, when it had gone on for some little time. "I have left my wise old grandfather, my brothers and my home, so that I might be in quiet and remember the truth—and here am I wasting my time with this horned imp of mischief!"

But as he had come out in a good cause, he nevertheless thought it the right thing to stay where he was.

III

So Quest and the goblin lived together on that lone ledge between the cliffs, and each day was like the first. The goblin worried Quest so that he couldn't get on with his thinking.

On a clear morning Quest would rise from sleep and feel happy. "How still it is, how lovely! Surely to-day I shall remember the truth!" And lo, from the branch overhead a handful of crabs would come tumbling about his ears, so that his head buzzed and his thoughts all got mixed. And there was the little monster mocking him from the crabtree and laughing fit to burst. Or Quest would be lying in the shade, thinking most beautifully, till he felt like saying: "There, there now, *now* it will come back to me, *now* I shall puzzle out the truth!" And then the goblin would squirt him all over with ice-cold water from the spring through a hollow elder twig—and again Quest would clean forget what he had already thought out.

There was no silly trick nor idle joke that the goblin did not play on Quest on the ledge there. And yet all might have been well, if Quest hadn't found it just a tiny bit amusing to watch these tomfooleries; and though he was think-

12

ing hard about his task, yet his eyes *would* wander and look round to see what the imp might be doing next.

Quest was angry with himself over this, because he was wearying more and more for his grandfather, and he saw full well that he would never remember the truth while the goblin was about.

"I must get rid of him," said Quest.

Well, one fine morning the goblin invented a new game. He climbed up the cliff where there was a steep water-course in the face of the rock, got astride a smooth bit of wood as if it had been a hobby-horse, and then scooted down the water-course like a streak of lightning! This prank pleased the little wretch so mightily that he must needs have company to enjoy it the better! So he whistled on a blade of grass till it rang over hill and dale, and lo, from scrub and rock and osier clump the goblins came scuttling along, all tiny like himself. He gave orders, and every man-jack of them took a stick and shinned up the cliff with it. My word! how they got astride their hobby-horses and hurtled down the water-course! There were all sorts and sizes and kinds of goblins—red as a robin's breast, green as greenfinches, woolly as lambs, naked as frogs, horned as snails, bald as mice. They careered down the water-course like a crazy company on crazy horses. Down they flew, each close at the other's heels, never stopping till they came to the middle of the ledge; and there was a great stone all overgrown with moss. There they were brought up short, and what with the bump of stopping so suddenly and sheer high spirits they tumbled and scrambled about all atop of one another in the moss!

Shrieking with glee, the silly crew had made the trip some two or three times already, and poor Quest was hard put to it between two thoughts. For one thing, he wanted to watch the imps and be amused by them, and for another he was angry with them for making such a hullabaloo that he could not remember the truth. So he shilly-shallied awhile, and at last he said: "Well, this is past a joke. I must get rid of these good-for-nothing loons, because while they are here I might as well have stopped at home."

And as Quest considered the matter, he noticed that as they rushed down the water-course they made straight for the spring, and that, but for the big stone, they would all have toppled into it head foremost. So Quest crouched behind the stone, and when the imps came dashing down again guffawing and chuckling as before, he quickly rolled the stone aside, and the whole mad party rushed straight on to the well-spring—right on to it and then into it, head first, each on top of the other—red as robin's breasts, green as greenfinches, woolly as lambs, naked as frogs, horned as snails, bald-headed as mice—and first of all the one who had fastened himself on to Quest....

And then Quest tipped a big flat stone over the well, and all the goblins were caught inside like flies in a pitcher.

Quest was ever so pleased to have got rid of the goblins, sat down and made sure he would now recollect the truth in good earnest.

But he had no luck, because down in the well the goblins began to wriggle and to ramp as never before. Through every gap and chink shot up tiny flames which the goblins gave out in their fright and distress. The flames danced and wavered round the spring till Quest's head was all in a whirl. He closed his eyes, so that their flashing should not make him giddy.

But then there arose from the pit such a noise, hubbub, knocking and banging, barking and yowling, such yelling and shrieking for help, that Quest's ears were like to burst; and how could he even try to think through it? He stopped his ears so as not to hear.

Then a smell of brimstone and sulphur drifted over to him. Through every crack and crevice oozed thick sooty smoke which the imps belched forth in their extremity. Smoke and sulphur fumes writhed round Quest; they choked and smothered him.

So Quest saw there was no help for it. "Goblins shut up," said he, "are a hundred times worse than goblins at large. So I'll just go and let them out, since I can't get rid of them anyhow. After all, I am better off with their tomfooleries than with all that yammering."

So he went and lifted off the stone; and the terrified goblins scuttled away in all directions like so many wild cats, and ran away into the woods and never came back to the ledge any more.

None stayed behind, but only the one black as a mole and with big horns, because he did not dare to leave Quest for fear of Rampogusto.

But even he sobered down a little from that day forward, and had more respect for Quest than before.

And so these two came to a sort of arrangement between them; they got used to one another and lived side by side on the stony ledge.

In that way close on to a year slipped by, and Quest was no nearer remembering what All-Rosy had really truly told him.

When the year was almost gone the goblin began to be most horribly bored.

"How much longer have I got to stick here?" thought he. So one evening, just as Quest was about to fall asleep, the imp wriggled up to him and said:

"Well, my friend, here you've been sitting for close on a year and a day, and what's the good of it? Who knows but perhaps in the meantime your old grand-dad has died all alone in his cabin."

A pang shot through Quest's heart as if he had been struck with a knife, but he said: "There, I have made up my mind not to budge from here until I remember the truth, because truth comes before all things." Thus said Quest, because he was upright and of good parts.

But all the same he was deeply troubled by what the goblin had said about his grandfather. He never slept a wink all night, but racked his brains and thought: "How is it with the old man, my dear grandfather?"

IV

Now all this time the grandfather went on living with Careful and Bluster in the glade—only life had taken a very sad turn for the old man. His grandsons ceased to trouble about him, nor would they stay near him. They bade him neither "Good-morning" nor "Good-night," and only went about their own affairs and listened to the goblins they harboured, the one in his pouch and the other in his bosom.

Every day Careful brought more bees from the forest, felled timber, shaped rafters, and gradually built a new cabin. He carved himself ten tallies, and every day he counted and reckoned over and over again when these tallies would be filled up.

As for Bluster, he went hunting and reiving, bringing home game and furs, plunder and treasure; and one day he even brought along two slaves whom he had taken, so that they might work for the brothers and wait upon them.

All this was very hard and disagreeable for the old man, and harder and more disagreeable still were the looks he got from his grandsons. What use had they for an old man who would not be served by the slaves, but disgraced his grandsons by cutting wood and drawing water from the well for himself? At last there wasn't a thing about the old man that didn't annoy his grandsons, even this, that every day he would put a log on the sacred fire.

Old Witting saw very well whither all this would lead, and that very soon they would be thinking of getting rid of him altogether. He did not care so much about his life, because life was not much use to him, but he was sorry to die before seeing Quest once more, the dear lad who was the joy of his old age.

One evening—and it was the very evening when Quest was so troubled in his mind thinking of his grandfather—Careful said to Bluster: "Come along, brother, let's get rid of grandfather. You have weapons. Wait for him by the well and kill him."

Now Careful said this because he specially wanted the old cabin at all costs, so as to put up beehives on that spot. "I can't," replied Bluster, whose heart had not grown so hard, amidst bloodshed and robbery, as Careful's among his riches and his tallies.

But Careful would not give over, because the imp in his bag went on whispering and nagging. The imp in his pouch knew very well that Careful would be the first to put the old man away, and so gain him great credit with Rampogusto.

Careful tried hard to talk over Bluster, but Bluster could not bring himself to kill his grandfather with his own hand. So at last they agreed and arranged that they would that very night burn down the old man's hut—burn it down with the old man inside!

When all was quiet in the glade, they sent out the slaves to watch the traps in the woods that night. But the brothers crept up softly to Witting's cabin, shut the outer door tight with a thick wedge, so that the old man might not escape from the flames, and then set fire to the four corners of the house....

When all was done they went away and away into the hills so as not to hear their poor old grandfather crying out for help. They made up their minds to go over the whole of the mountain as far as they could, and not to come back until next day, when all would be over, and their grandfather and the cabin would be burnt up together.

So they went, and the flames began to lick upwards slowly round the corners. But the rafters were of seasoned walnut, hard as stone, and though the fire licked and crept all round them it could not catch properly, and so it was late at night before the flames took hold of the roof.

Old Witting awoke, opened his eyes and saw that the roof was ablaze over his head. He got up and went to the door, and when he found that it was fastened with a heavy wedge he knew at once whose doing it was.

"Oh, my children! my poor darlings!" said the old man, "you have taken from your hearts to add to your wretched tallies; and behold, your tallies are not even full, and there are many notches still lacking; but your hearts are empty to the bottom already, since you could burn your own grandfather and the cabin where you were born."

That was all the thought that Father Witting gave to Careful and Bluster. After that he thought neither good nor bad about them, nor did he grieve over them further, but went and sat down quietly to wait for death.

He sat on the oak chest and meditated upon his long life; and whatever there had been in it, there was nothing he was sorry for save only this, that Quest was not with him in his last hour—Quest, his darling child, for whom he had grieved so much.

So he sat still, while the roof was already blazing away like a torch.

The rafters burned and burned, the ceiling began to crack. It blazed, cracked, then gave way on either side of the old man, and rafters and ceiling crashed down amid the flames into the cabin. The flames billowed round Witting, the roof gaped above his head. Already he saw the dawn pale in the sky before sunrise. Old Witting rose to his feet, raised his hands to heaven, and so waited for the flames to carry him away from this world, the old man and his old homestead together.

V

Quest worried terribly that night, and when morning broke he went to the spring to cool his burning face.

The sun was just up in the sky when Quest reached the spring, and when he came there he saw a light shining in the water. It shone, it rose, and lo! beside the spring and before Quest stood a lovely youth in golden raiment. It was All-Rosy.

Quest started with joy, and said:

"My little lord All-Rosy bright, how I have longed for you! Do tell me what you told me then that I must do? Here I have been racking my brains and tormenting myself and calling on all my wits for a year and a day—and I cannot remember the truth!"

As Quest said this, All-Rosy rather crossly shook his head and his golden curls.

"Eh, boy, boy! I told you to stay with your grandfather till you had rendered him the love you owe him, and not to leave him till he left you," said All-Rosy.

And then he went on:

"I thought you were wiser than your brothers, and there you are the most foolish of the three. Here you have been racking your brains and calling on your wits to help you for a year and a day so that you might remember the truth; and if you had listened to your heart when it told you on the threshold of your cabin to turn back and not to leave your old grandfather—why then, you silly boy, you would have had the truth, even without wits!"

Thus spoke All-Rosy. Once more he crossly shook his head with the golden curls; then he took his golden cloak about him and vanished.

Shamed and troubled, Quest remained alone beside the spring, and from between the stones he heard the imp giggling—the hobgoblin, quite small, misshapen, and horned with big horns. The little wretch was pleased because All-Rosy had shamed Quest, who always gave himself such righteous airs; but when Quest roused himself from his first amazement he called out joyfully:

"Now I'll just wash quickly and then fly to my dear old grandfather." This he said and knelt by the spring to wash. Quest leaned down to reach the water, leaned down too far, lost his balance, and fell into the spring.

Fell into the spring and was drowned....

VI

The hobgoblin jumped up from among the stones, leaped to the edge of the spring, and looked down to see with his own eyes whether it was really true.

Yes, Quest was really truly drowned. There he lay at the bottom of the water, white as wax.

"Yoho, yoho, yo hey!" yelled the goblin, who was only a poor silly. "Yoho, yoho, yo hey! my friend, we're off to-day!"

The imp yelled so that all the rocks round the ledge rang with the noise. Then he heaved up the stone that lay by the edge of the spring, and the stone toppled over and covered the spring like a lid. Next the imp flung Quest's skin-coat on the top of the stone; last of all he went and sat on the coat, and then he began to skip and to frolic.

"Yoho, yoho! my job is done!" yelled the goblin.

But it wasn't for long that he skipped on the skin; it wasn't for long that he yelled.

For when the goblin had tired himself out, he looked round the ledge, and a queer feeling came over him.

You see, the goblin had got used to Quest. Never before had he had such an easy time as with that good youth. He had been allowed to fool about as he chose, without anybody scolding him or telling him to stop; and now that he came to think of it, he would have to go back to the osier clump, to the mire, to his angry King Rampogusto, and go on repeating the old goblin chatter among five hundred other goblins—all of them just as he used to be himself.

He had lost the habit of it. He began to think—to *think* a very little. He began to feel sad—just a little sad, then more and more miserable; and at last he was wringing and beating his hands, and the silly, thoughtless goblin, who a minute ago had been yelling with glee, was now weeping and wailing with grief and rolling about on the coat all crazy with distress.

He wept and he howled till all his former yelling was clean nothing in comparison. For a goblin is always a goblin. Once he starts wailing he wails with a vengeance. And he pulled the fur out of the skin-coat in handfuls, and rolled about on it as if he had taken leave of his senses.

Now just at that moment Bluster and Careful came to the lone ledge.

They had wandered all over the mountain, and were now on their way home to the glade to see if their grandfather and the cabin were quite burnt up. On the way back they came to a lone ledge where they had never been before.

Bluster and Careful heard something wailing, and caught sight of Quest's skin-coat; and they thought at once that Quest must have come to grief somehow.

Not that they felt sorry for their brother because they could not grieve for anybody while the goblins were about them.

But at that moment their goblins began to wriggle, because they could hear that one of their own kind was in trouble. Now there is no sort that sticks more closely together and none more faithful in trouble than the hobgoblins were. In the osier clump they would fight and squabble all day; but if there was trouble each would give the skin off his shins for the other!

So they wriggled and they worried; they pricked up their ears, and then peered out, the one from the pouch and the other from the shirt. And as they peered they at once saw a brother of theirs rolling about with somebody or something—rolling and writhing, and nothing to be seen but the fur flying.

"A wild beast is worrying him!" cried the terrified goblins. They jumped out, one out of Careful's pouch and the other out of Bluster's bosom, and scuttled off to help their friend.

But when they reached him, he would still do nothing but roll about on the skin and howl:

"The boy is dead!—the boy is dead!" The other two goblins tried to quiet him, and thought: "Maybe a thorn has got into his paw, or a midge into his

19

ear"—because they had never lived with a righteous man, and did not know what it means to lament for others.

But the first goblin went on wailing so that you couldn't hear yourself speak, and he wouldn't be comforted either.

So the other goblins were in a fine taking as to what they were to do with him? Nor could they leave him there in his sore trouble. At last they had an idea. Each laid hold of the sheep-skin coat by one sleeve, and so they dragged along the coat with their brother inside, scuttled away into the woods, and out of the woods into the osier clump and home to Rampogusto.

So for the first time for a year and a day Bluster and Careful were quit of their goblins. When the imps hopped away from them, the brothers felt as though they had walked the world like blind men for a year and a day, and were seeing it plainly again now for the first time there on the rocky ledge.

First they looked at each other in a maze, and then they knew at once what a terrible wrong they had done their grandfather.

"Brother! kinsman!" each cried to the other, "let us fly and save our grand-father." And they flew as if they had falcon's wings, home to the clearing.

When they came to the glade the cabin was roofless. Flames were rising like a column from the hut. Only the walls and the door were still standing, and the door was still tightly wedged.

The brothers hurried up, tore out the wedge, rushed into the cabin, and carried out the old man in their arms from amid the flames, which were just going to take hold on his feet.

They carried him out and laid him on the cool green turf, and then they stood beside him and neither dared speak a word.

After a while old Witting opened his eyes, and as he saw them he asked nothing about them. The only question he put was:

"Did you find Quest anywhere in the mountain?"

"No, grandfather," answered the brothers. "Quest is dead. He was drowned this morning in the well-spring. But, grandfather, forgive us, and we will serve you and wait upon you like slaves."

As they were speaking thus, old Witting arose and stood upon his feet.

"I see that you are already forgiven, my children," said he, "since you are standing here alive. But he who was the most upright of you three had to pay with his life for his fault. Come, children, take me to the place where he died."

Humbly penitent, Careful and Bluster supported their grandfather as they led him to the ledge.

But when they had walked a little while they saw that they had gone astray, and had never been that way before. They told their grandfather; but he just bade them keep on in that path.

So they came to a steep slope, and the road led up the slope right to the crest of the mountain.

"Our grandfather will die," whispered the brothers, "with him so feeble and the hillside so steep."

But old Witting only said: "On, children, on—follow the path."

20

So they began to climb up the track, and the old man grew ever more grey and pallid in the face. And on the mountain's crest there was something fair that rustled and crooned and sparkled and shone.

And when they reached the crest, they stood silent and stone still for very wonder and awe.

For before them was neither hill nor dale, nor mountain nor plain, nor anything at all, but only a great white cloud stretched out before them like a great white sea—a white cloud, and on the white cloud a pink cloud. Upon the pink cloud stood a glass mountain, and on the glass mountain a golden castle with wide steps leading up to the gates.

That was the Golden Castle of All-Rosy. A soft light streamed from the Castle—some of it from the pink cloud, some from the glass mountain, and some from the pure gold walls; but most of all from the windows of the Castle itself. For there sit the guests of All-Rosy, drinking from golden goblets health and welcome to each new-comer.

But All-Rosy does not enjoy the company of such as harbour any guilt in their souls, nor will he let them into his Castle. Wherefore it is a noble and chosen company that is assembled in his courts, and from them streams the light through the windows.

Upon the ridge stood old Witting with his grandsons, all speechless as they gazed at the marvel. They looked—and of a sudden they saw someone sitting on the steps that led to the Castle. His face was hidden in his hands and he wept.

The old man looked and knew him—knew him for Quest.

The old man's soul was shaken within him. He roused himself and called out across the cloud:

"What ails you, my child?"

"I am here, grandfather," answered Quest. "A great light lifted me up out of the well-spring and brought me here. So far have I come; but they won't let me into the Castle, because I have sinned against you."

Tears ran down the old man's cheeks. His hands and heart went out to caress his dear child, to comfort him, to help him, to set his darling free.

Careful and Bluster looked at their grandfather, but his face was altogether changed. It was ashen, it was haggard, and not at all like the face of a living man.

"The old man will die of these terrors," whispered the brothers to each other.

But the old man drew himself up to his full height, and already he was moving away from them, when he looked back once more and said:

"Go home, children, back to the glade, since you are forgiven. Live and enjoy in all righteousness what shall fall to your part. But I go to help him to whom has been given the best part at the greatest cost."

Old Witting's voice was quite faint, but he stood before them upright as a dart.

Bluster and Careful looked at one another. Had their grandfather gone crazy, that he thought of walking across the clouds when he had no breath even for speech?

But already the old man had left them. He left them, went on and stepped out upon the cloud as though it were a meadow. And as he stepped out he went forward. On he walked, the old man, and his feet carried him as though

he were a feather, and his cloak fluttered in the wind as if it were a cloud upon that cloud. Thus he came to the pink cloud, and to the glass mountain, and
to the broad steps. He flew up the steps to his grandson. Oh the joy of it,
when the old man clasped his grandson! He hugged him and he held him
close as if he would never let him go. And Careful and Bluster heard it all.
Across the cloud they could hear the old man and his grandchild weeping in
each other's arms for pure joy!

Then the old man took Quest by the hand and led him up to the Castle
gates. With his left hand he led his grandson, and with his right he knocked at
the gate.

And lo, a wonder! At once the great gates flew open, all the splendour of
the Castle was thrown open, and the company within, the noble guests, welcomed grandfather Witting and grandson Quest upon the threshold.

They welcomed them, held out their hands to them, and led them in.

Careful and Bluster just saw them pass by the window, and saw where
they were placed at the table. The first place of all was given to old Witting,
and beside him sat Quest, where All-Rosy, the golden youth, drinks welcome
to his guests from a goblet of gold.

A great fear fell upon Bluster and Careful when they were left alone with
these awesome sights.

"Come away, brother, to our clearing," whispered Careful; and they turned
and went. Bewildered by many marvels, they got back to their clearing, and
never again could they find either the path or the slope that led to the mountain's crest.

VII

Thus it was and thus it befell.

Careful and Bluster went on living in the glade. They lived long as valiant
men and true, and brought up goodly families, sons and grandsons. All good
parts went down from father to son, and, of course, also the sacred fire,
which was fed with a fresh log every day so that it might never go out.

So, you see, Rampogusto was right in being afraid of Quest, because if
Quest had not died in his search for truth those goblins would never have left
Careful and Bluster, and in the glade there would have been neither right-
eous men nor sacred fire.

But so everything fell out. To the great shame and discomfiture of Rampogusto and all his crew.

When those two goblins dragged Quest's sheep-skin before Rampogusto,
and inside it the third goblin, who was still yammering and carrying on like
one demented, Rampogusto flew into a furious rage, for he knew that all
three youths had escaped him. In his great wrath he gave orders that all
three goblins should have their horns cropped close, and so run about for
everyone to make fun of!

But the worst of Rampogusto's discomfiture was this: Every day the sacred smoke gets into his throat and makes him cough most horribly. Moreover, he never dare venture out into the woods for fear of meeting some one of the valiant people.

So Rampogusto got nothing out of it but Quest's cast-off sheep-skin; and I'm sure he is welcome to that, for Quest doesn't want a sheep-skin coat anyhow in All-Rosy's Golden Halls.

Fisherman Plunk and His Wife

FISHERMAN PLUNK was sick and tired of his miserable life. He lived alone by the desolate sea-shore, and every day he caught fish with a bone hook, because they didn't know about nets in those parts at that time. And how much fish can you catch with a hook, anyhow?

"What a dog's life it is, to be sure!" cried Plunk to himself. "What I catch in the morning I eat up at night, and there's no joy for me in this world at all, at all."

And then Plunk heard that there were also rich sheriffs in the land, and men of great power and might, who lived in luxury and comfort, lapped in gold and fed on truffles. Then Plunk fell a-thinking how he too might come to look upon such riches and live in the midst of them. So he made up his mind that for three whole days he would sit still in his boat on the sea and not take any fish at all, but see if that spell would help him.

So Plunk sat for three days and nights in his boat on the face of the sea—three days he sat there, three days he fasted, for three days he caught no fish. When the third day began to dawn, lo and behold, a silver boat arose from the sea—a silver boat with golden oars—and in the boat, fair as a king's daughter, stood the Pale Dawn-Maiden.

"For three days you have spared my little fishes' lives," said the Dawn-Maiden, "and now tell me what you would like me to do for you?"

"Help me out of this miserable and dreary life. Here am I all day long slaving away in this desolate place. What I catch during the day I eat up at night, and there is no joy for me in the world at all, at all," said Plunk.

"Go home," said the Dawn-Maiden, "and you will find what you need." And as she spoke, she sank in the sea, silver boat and all.

Plunk hurried back to the shore and then home. When he came to the house, a poor orphan girl came out to meet him, all weary with the long tramp across the hills. The girl said: "My mother is dead, and I am all alone in the world. Take me for your wife, Plunk."

Plunk hardly knew what to do. "Is this the good fortune which the Dawn-Maiden has sent me?" Plunk could see that the girl was just a poor body like himself; on the other hand, he was afraid of making a mistake and turning away his luck. So he consented, and took the poor girl to be his wife; and she, being very tired, lay down and slept till the morning.

Plunk could scarcely await the next day for wondering how his good fortune would show itself. But nothing happened that day except that Plunk took his hook and went out fishing, and the Woman went up the hill to gather wild spinach. Plunk came home at night, and so did the Woman, and they supped upon fish and wild spinach. "Eh, if that is all the good luck there is to it, I could just as well have done without," thought Plunk.

As the evening wore on, the Woman sat down beside Plunk to tell him stories, to wile away the time for him. She told him about nabobs and kings' castles, about dragons that watch treasure-hoards, and kings' daughters who sow their gardens with pearls and reap gems. Plunk listened, and his heart within him began to sing for joy. Plunk forgot that he was poor; he could have sat and listened to her for three years together. But Plunk was still better pleased when he considered: "She is a fairy wife. She can show me the way to the dragons' hoards or the kings' gardens. I need only be patient and not make her angry."

So Plunk waited; and day after day went by, a year went by, two years passed. A little son was born to them; they called him little Winpeace. Yet all went on as usual. Plunk caught fish, and his wife gathered wild spinach in the mountains. In the evening she cooked the supper, and after supper she rocked the baby and told Plunk stories. Her stories grew prettier and prettier, and Plunk found it harder and harder to wait, till at last, one evening, he had had enough of it; and just as his wife was telling him about the immense treasures of the Sea King, Plunk jumped up in a rage, shook her by the arm and cried:

"I tell you I'll wait no longer. To-morrow in the morning you shall take me down to the Sea King's Castle!"

The Woman was quite frightened when Plunk jumped up like that. She told him that she did not know where the Sea King had his Castle; but Plunk began to beat his poor wife most unmercifully, and threatened to kill her unless she told him her fairy secret.

Then the poor girl understood that Plunk had taken her for a fairy. She burst into tears and cried:

"Truly I am no fairy, but a poor orphan girl who knows no spells nor magic. And for the tales I have told you, I had them from my own heart to beguile your weariness."

Now this only put Plunk all the more in a rage, because he had lived in a fool's paradise for over two years; and he angrily bade the Woman go away next morning ere dawn with the child, along the sea-shore to the right-hand side, and he, Plunk, would go to the left, and she was not to come back again till she had found the way to the Sea King's Castle.

When the dawn came, the Woman wept and begged Plunk not to send her away. "Who knows where one of us may be destroyed on this desolate sea-shore?" said she. But Plunk fell upon her again, so that she took up her child and went away crying whither her husband had bidden her. And Plunk went off in the opposite direction.

So the Woman went on with her baby, little Winpeace. She went on for a week; she went on for a fortnight, and nowhere did she find the way to the Sea King. She grew so terribly tired that one day she fell asleep on a stone beside the sea. When she woke up, her baby was gone—her little Winpeace.

Her grief was so great that the tears froze fast in her heart, and not a word could she speak for sorrow, but became dumb from that hour.

So the poor dumb creature wandered back along the sea-shore and home. And next day Plunk came home, too. He had not found the way to the Sea King, and he came back disappointed and cross.

When he got home, there was no baby Winpeace, and his wife had gone dumb. She could not tell him what had happened, but was all haggard with the great trouble.

And so it was with them from that day forward. The Woman neither wept nor complained, but did her housework and waited upon Plunk in silence; and the house was still and quiet as the grave. For some time Plunk stood it, but in the end he got thoroughly weary. He had just felt almost sure of the Sea King's treasure, and lo! all this trouble and worry had come upon him.

So Plunk made up his mind to try his sea-spell once more. Again for three whole days he sat in his boat on the sea, for three days he fasted, for three days he caught no fish. At the third day, at daybreak, the Dawn-Maiden arose before him.

Plunk told her what had happened, and complained bitterly.

"I'm worse off than ever before. The baby is gone, the wife is dumb, and my house dreary as the grave, and I'm just about bursting with trouble."

To this the Dawn-Maiden said never a word, but just asked Plunk a question:

"What do you want? I will help you just this once more."

But Plunk was such a zany that he couldn't think of anything else but just this, that he was set on seeing and enjoying the Sea King's treasure; and so he didn't wish for his child back again, or that his wife should regain the power of speech, but he begged the Dawn-Maiden:

"Fair Dawn-Maiden," said he, "show me the way to the Sea King."

And again the Dawn-Maiden said nothing, but very kindly set Plunk on his way:

"When day dawns at the next New Moon, get into your boat, wait for the wind, and then drift eastward with the wind. The wind will carry you to the Isle Bountiful, to the stone Gold-a-Fire. And there I shall be waiting for you to show you the way to the Sea King."

Plunk went joyfully home.

When it was about the New Moon (but he never told his wife anything) he went out at the streak of dawn, got into his boat, waited for the wind, and let the wind carry him away toward the east.

The wind caught the boat and carried it along to the Unknown Sea, to the Isle Bountiful. Like a green garden the fruitful island floats upon the sea. The grass grows rank, and the meadows lush, the vines are full of grapes and the almondtrees pink with blossom. In the midst of the island there is precious stone, the white blazing stone Gold-a-Fire. One half of the stone sheds its glow upon the island, and the other half lights up the sea under the island. And there on the Isle Bountiful, on the stone Gold-a-Fire, sits the Dawn-Maiden.

Very kindly did the Dawn-Maiden receive Plunk, very kindly she set him on his way. She showed him a mill-wheel drifting on the sea towards the island, and the mermaids dancing in a ring around the wheel. Then she told him— always very kindly—how he must ask the mill-wheel politely to take him down to the Sea King and not let the Dark Deeps of the Sea swallow him.

Last of all the Dawn-Maiden said:

"Great store of gold and treasure will you enjoy in the Sea King's domain. But mark—to earth you cannot return, for three terrible watchers bar the way. One troubles the waves, the second raises the storm, and the third wields the lightning."

But Plunk was happy as a grig in his boat as he paddled towards the mill-wheel, and thought to himself:

"It's easy to see, fair Dawn-Maiden, that you've never known want in this world. I shan't hanker back after this earth, where I'm leaving nothing but ill-luck behind!"

So he paddled up to the mill-wheel, where round the mill-wheel the mermaids were playing their foolish games. They dived and chased each other through the water; their long hair floated on the waves, their silver fins glittered, and their red lips smiled. And they sat on the mill-wheel and made the sea all foamy around it.

The boat reached the mill-wheel, and Plunk did as the Dawn-Maiden had told him. He held his paddle aloft so that the Dark Deeps should not swallow him, and he politely asked the mill-wheel:

"Round wheel giddy-go-round, please take me down, either to the Dead Dark Deep or to the Sea King's Palace."

As Plunk said this, the mermaids came swishing along like so many silver fish, swarmed round the mill-wheel, seized the spokes in their snowy hands, and began to turn the wheel—swiftly, giddily.

An eddy formed in the sea—a fierce eddy, a terrible whirlpool. The whirlpool caught Plunk; it swept him round like a twig, and sucked him down to the Sea King's fastness.

Plunk's ears were still ringing with the swirl of the sea and the mermaids' silly laughter when he suddenly found himself sitting on beautiful sand—fine sand of pure gold.

Plunk looked round and cried out: "Ho, there's a wonder for you! A whole field of golden sand."

Now what Plunk had taken to be a big field was only the great Hall of the Sea King. Round the Hall stood the sea like a marble wall, and above the Hall hung the sea, like a glass dome. Down from the stone Gold-a-Fire streamed a bluish glare, livid and pale as moonlight. From the ceiling hung festoons of pearls, and on the floor below stood tables of coral.

And at the end—the far end, where slender pipes were piping and tiny bells tinkling—there lazed and lounged the Sea King himself; he stretched his limbs on the golden sand, raising only his great bullock's head, beside him a coral table, and behind him a golden hedge.

What with the quick, shrill music of the pipes, the tinkling of the bells, and the sheen and glimmer all around him, Plunk wouldn't have believed there could be so much pleasure or wealth in the world!

Plunk went clean mad for pure joy—joy went to his head like strong wine; his heart sang; he clapped his hands; he skipped about the golden sand like a frolicsome child; he turned head over heels once, twice, and again—just like a jolly boy.

Now this amused the Sea King vastly. For the Sea King's feet are heavy—far too heavy—and his great bullock's head is heavier still. The Sea King guffawed as he lounged on the golden sand; he laughed so heartily that the golden sand blew up all round him.

"You're fine and light on your feet, my boy," said the Sea King, and he reached up and pulled down a branch of pearls and gave it to Plunk. And then the Sea King ordered the Under Seas Fairies to bring choice viands and honeyed drink in golden vessels. And Plunk had leave to sit beside the Sea King at the coral table, and surely that was a great honour!

When Plunk had dined, the Sea King asked him:

"Is there anything else you would like, my man?"

Now what should a poor man ask for, who had never known what it is to have a good time? But Plunk was hungry from his long journey, and he had made but a poor meal of it off the choice viands and the honeyed drinks. So he said to the Sea King:

"Just as you were saying that, O King of the Sea, I was wishing that I had a good helping of boiled wild spinach."

The Sea King was rather surprised, but he recovered himself quickly, laughed and said to Plunk:

"Eh, brother of mine, wild spinach is very dear down here, dearer than pearls and mother-o'-pearl, because it's a long way from here to the place where it grows. But since you have just asked for it, I will send a Foam Fairy to bring you some from the land where the wild spinach grows. But you must turn three more coach-wheels for me."

As Plunk was already in the best of humours he didn't find that hard either. Lightly he leapt to his feet, and quickly they all flocked round him, the mermaids and the tiny folk in the Palace, and all for to see that wonder!

Plunk took a run over the golden sand, turned a beautiful coach-wheel, then a second and a third, light as a squirrel, and the Sea King and all the tiny folk rocked with laughter at such cunning.

But heartiest of all laughed a little baby, and that was the little King whom the mermaids themselves had crowned King for fun and idle sport. The wee baby was sitting up in a golden cradle. His little shirt was of silk, the cradle was hung with tiny bells of pearl, and in his hands the child held a golden apple.

While Plunk was turning coach-wheels and the little King laughed so heartily, Plunk looked round at him. He looked at the little King, and then—Plunk started. It was his own baby boy, little Winpeace.

Well, Plunk was suddenly disgusted. He would never have guessed that he would grow sick of it so soon.

Plunk frowned; he was angry, and when he had got over his shock a bit he thought:

"Look at him, the urchin, how he's got on, lording it here in idleness and sport, and his mother at home gone dumb with grieving!"

Plunk was vexed; he hated seeing himself or the child in this Palace; yet he dared not say a word, lest they should part him from the boy. So he made himself the servant of his son, of little Winpeace, and thought to himself: "Perhaps I shall be left alone with him sometimes. Then I will remind the boy of his Father and Mother; I will run away with him; I will carry off the little brat and go back with him to his mother."

So thought Plunk, and one fine day, when he happened to be alone with the little King, he whispered to the child: "Come along, my boy; let's run away with father."

But Winpeace was only a baby, and what with living so long under the sea, he had quite forgotten his father. He laughed; the little King laughed. He thought: "Plunk is making fun," and he kicked Plunk with his little foot.

"You are not my father; you are the silly-billy who turns head over heels before the Sea King."

That stung Plunk to the heart, so that he well-nigh died with the pain of it. He went out and wept for sheer bitter sorrow. All the Sea King's attendants gathered round him and said one to the other:

"Well, well, he must have been a great lord on earth, to weep amid such splendours."

"Upon my soul," cried Plunk wrathfully, "I was the same as your Sea King here. I had a son who tugged my beard, a wife who showed me marvels, and wild spinach, brothers, as much as you want—and no need to turn coach-wheels before anybody either."

The sea-folk marvelled at such magnificence, and left Plunk to mourn his lost greatness. But Plunk went on serving the little King. He did all he could to please the boy, thinking: "I shall get him somehow to run away with me." But the little King grew sillier and more wayward every day; the days passed, and every day the child only thought Plunk more than ever a zany.

II

Now all this time Plunk's wife was at home, all alone and grieving. The first evening she made up the fire and kept the supper hot for Plunk; but when she gave up expecting Plunk, she let the fire go out, nor did she kindle it again.

So the poor dumb soul sat on her threshold. She neither worked, nor tidied, nor wept, nor lamented, but just pined away with grief and sorrow. She could not take counsel with anyone, because she was dumb; nor could she cross the sea after Plunk, because she was all broken up with grieving.

Where could she go, poor soul! but back one day to the far hills, where her mother lay buried. And as she stood by her mother's grave a beautiful Hind up came to her.

And as the dumb animals speak, so the Hind spoke to the Woman:

"You must not sit there and pine away, my daughter, for else your heart will break and your house will perish. But every evening you must get Plunk's supper ready for him, and after supper you must unpick some fine hemp. If Plunk does not come home, then you must take his supper in the morning and the fine hemp as well, and also the slender twin pipes, and go up into the rocky mountain. Play upon the twin pipes; the snakes and their young will come and eat up the supper, and the sea-fowl will line their nests with the hemp."

Full well the daughter understood all that her mother said, and as she was bid so did she do. Every evening she cooked supper, and after supper she unpicked hemp. Plunk did not come back; and so the Woman took her little twin pipes in the morning, and carried both supper and hemp to the rocky mountain. And as she played on her little pipes, played softly on the right-hand pipe, lo, snakes and baby snakes came out of the rocks. They ate up the supper and thanked the Woman in the dumb speech. And when she played on the left-hand pipe, lo, gulls great and small came flying, carried off the hemp to their nests, and thanked the Woman.

For three months the Woman went on in this way; thrice the moon waxed and waned, and still Plunk had not come home.

Again grief overcame the poor dumb soul, so that she went again to her mother's grave.

The Hind came up, and in dumb speech the Woman said to her:

"Well, Mother, I have done all you told me, and Plunk has not come back. I am weary of waiting. Shall I throw myself into the sea, or fling myself down from the cliffs?"

"Daughter of mine," said the Hind, "you must not fail in your trust. Your Plunk is in grievous trouble. Now listen and hear how you may help him. In the Unknown Sea there is a Big Bass, and that Bass has a golden fin, and on that fin grows a golden apple. If you catch that Bass by moonlight you will deliver your dear Plunk from his trouble. But on the road to the Unknown Sea you will have to pass three caverns of cloud. In the first there is a monstrous Snake, the Mother of All Snakes—it is she who troubles the sea and stirs up the waves; in the second there is a monstrous Bird, the Mother of All Birds—it is she who raises the storm; and in the third there is a Golden Bee—it is she who flashes and wields the lightning. Go, daughter dear, to the Unknown Sea, and take nothing with you but your bone hook and slender twin pipes, and if you should find yourself in great trouble, rip open your right-hand sleeve, all white and unhemmed."

The daughter gave good heed. Next day she took out the boat and put off to sea, taking nothing with her but her hook and the slender twin pipes.

She drifted and sailed on the face of the sea till the waters bore her to a far-off place, and there on the sea, lo, three terrible caverns of lowering cloud!

From the entrance of the first cavern peered the head of a fearsome Snake, the Mother of All Snakes. Her grisly head blocked up all the entrance, her body lay coiled along the cave, and with her monstrous tail she lashed the sea, troubling the waters and stirring up the waves.

The Woman did not dare go near the terrible sight, but remembered her little pipes, and began to play upon the right-hand pipe. And as she played, there came from the far-off, rock-bound lands snakes and baby snakes galore swimming over the sea. Great coloured snakes and tiny little snakes all came hurrying up and scurrying up and begged the fearsome Snake—

"Let the Woman take her boat through your cavern, Mother dear! She has done us a great good turn and fed us every day in the morning."

"Through my cavern I may not let her pass," answered the fearsome Snake, "for to-day I must stir up the waves of the sea. But if she did you such a good turn, I will repay it with another. Would she rather have a bar of gold or six strings of pearls?"

But a true wife is not to be beguiled with gold or pearls, and so the Woman answered in dumb speech:

"'Tis only for a small matter I have come here—for the Bass that lives in the Unknown Sea. If I have done you a good turn, let me pass through your cavern, fearsome Snake."

"Let her pass, Mother dear," said the snakes and baby snakes again. "Here are many of us whom she has fed—full many to whom she gave meat. You just lie down, Mother dear, and take a nap, and we'll stir up the waters for you."

Now the Snake couldn't very well disoblige such a big family, and she had been longing for sleep for a thousand years. So she let the Woman through the cavern, and then curled up on the floor of the cavern and fell into a fear-

33

some sleep. But before she fell asleep she reminded the snakes and baby snakes once more:

"Now, stir me up the waters right properly, children dear, while I rest a little."

So the Woman passed through the cavern, and the snakes and their young stayed in the cavern; but instead of stirring up the sea they soothed it and made it calm.

The Woman sailed on, and came to the second cavern. And in the second cavern there was a monstrous Bird, the Mother of All Birds. She craned her frightful head through the opening, her iron beak gaped wide; she spread her vast wings in the cavern and flapped them, and whenever she flapped her wings she raised a storm.

The Woman took up her twin pipes and sweetly played upon the left-hand pipe. And from the far shore came flying gulls great and small, and begged the monstrous bird to let the Woman pass with her boat through her cavern, for that she had been a good friend to them and unpicked hemp for them every day.

"I can't let her pass through my cavern, for to-day I must raise a mighty storm. But if she was so kind to you, I will repay her with even greater kindness. From my iron beak I will give her of the Water of Life, so that the power of speech shall be restored to her."

Well, and wasn't it a sore temptation for the poor dumb creature who desired above all things that the power of speech should return to her? But she remained steadfast, and this is what she answered the Bird:

"'Tis not for my own good that I came, but for a small matter—for the Bass that lives in the Unknown Sea. If I have done you a good turn, let me pass through your cavern."

Then the grey gulls all entreated the Mother Bird and also advised her to take a little nap, and they would meanwhile raise the storm for her. The Mother Bird listened to her children's entreaty, clung to the wall of the cavern with her iron talons and went to sleep.

But the gulls great and small, instead of raising the storm, calmed the wild winds and soothed them.

So the dumb Woman sailed through the second cavern and came to the third.

In the third cavern she found the Golden Bee. The Golden Bee buzzed in the entrance; she wielded the fiery lightning and the rolling thunder. Sea and cavern resounded; lightnings flashed from the clouds.

Fear seized upon the Woman when she found herself all alone with these terrors. But she remembered her right sleeve; she ripped it off, her sleeve all white and unhemmed, flung it over the Golden Bee and caught her in the sleeve!

The thunder and lightning were stilled at once, and the Golden Bee began to coax the Woman:

"Set me free, O Woman! and in return I will show you something. Look out over the wide waters, and it's a joyful sight you will see."

The Woman looked out over the wide waters. The sun was just on the horizon. The sky grew pink overhead; the sea grew crimson from the east, and from the sea arose a silver boat. And in the boat sat the Dawn-Maiden, pale and fair as a king's daughter, and beside her a little child in a silken shirt and with a golden apple in his hand. It was the Dawn-Maiden taking the little King for his morning sail on the sea.

The Woman recognised her lost baby.

Now isn't that a wonder of wonders, that the sea should be so wide that a mother cannot encompass it, and the sun so high that a mother should not be able to reach it?

Her joy took hold of her like terror. She trembled like the slender aspen. Should she stretch out her hand to the child? or call to him tenderly? or should she just stand and look at him for ever and ever?

The silver boat glided over the crimson sea. It faded away in the distance; the boat sank under the waves, and the mother roused herself with a start.

"I will show you," said the Golden Bee to the Woman, "how to get to the little King, your son, and live with him in joy and happiness. But first set me free, that I may wield the lightnings in the cavern—and through my cavern I cannot let you pass!"

A fierce pang overcame the poor mother, overwhelmed and shook her. She had seen her darling; her eyes had beheld her heart's desire; she had seen and beheld him, but not hugged him, not kissed him! The pang shook her from head to foot. Should she be true to Plunk or no? Should she let the Bee

35

go and win to her child, or pass through the cavern to the Unknown Sea for the sake of the Big Bass?

But even as the pang shot through the Woman, the tears gushed forth from her heart; the power of speech returned to her, and 'twas in living words that she answered the Golden Bee:

"Don't sting me, O Golden Bee! I shall not let you go, because I must pass through your cavern. I have wept for my child and buried him in my heart. I have not come here for my own happiness, but for a small matter—for the Big Bass that lives in the Unknown Sea."

Thus said the Woman, and passed into the cavern. She rested in the cavern; she took her ease in the boat, and there she waited for nightfall and moon-rise.

Eh, my dearie, but the sea was quiet that day, with the winds at rest in the sky, and the fearsome Snake asleep in the first cavern, and the monstrous Bird asleep in the second, and the wearied Woman in the third!

So the day went quietly by; evening came, and the moon rose. When the moon rode high in the heavens, the Woman sailed out upon the Unknown Sea at midnight, and in the midst of the Sea she let down her little bone hook.

III

That very evening the little King bade Plunk knit him a nice set of silken reins. "First thing to-morrow morning I shall harness you to my little carriage, and you shall give me a ride on the golden sands."

Dearie me, considered poor Plunk, and where was he to hide from the Dawn-Maiden when she would go down into the sea in the morning and behold him thus to-morrow harnessed to a cart by his own son?

All the Sea King's court slept. The Sea King slept. The wilful little King slept—only Plunk was awake and knitting away at the reins. He knitted fiercely, like one who is thinking hard. When it seemed to him that the strings were strong enough, Plunk said to himself:

"I never asked anyone's counsel when I was making a fool of myself, nor shall I do so now that I have come to my senses."

And as he said this he went softly up to the cradle where his son lay fast asleep, wound the reins round and round the rockers of the cradle, lashed the cradle to his own back, and started to run away with his son.

Softly Plunk strode over the golden sand—strode through the mighty Hall, spacious as a wide meadow; slipped through the golden hedge, parting the branches of pearls; and when he came to where the sea stood up like a wall, nothing daunted, Plunk dived into the water with his boy.

But it is far—terribly far—from the Sea King's fastness to the world of day above! Plunk swam and swam; but how was a poor fisherman to swim when he was weighed down by the little King—golden cradle, golden apple and all—on his back?

36

Plunk felt as if the sea was piling itself up above him, higher and higher, and heavier and heavier!

And just as Plunk was at the last gasp, he felt something scrape along the golden cradle, something that caught in the rocker of the cradle; and when it had caught fast, it began to haul them along apace!

"Now it's all up with me!" said poor Plunk to himself. "Here's a sea-monster carrying me away on his tusk."

But it wasn't the tusk of a sea-monster; it was a bone fish-hook, the very hook that Plunk's wife had let down.

When the Woman felt that her hook had caught, she joyfully summoned all her strength, pulling and hauling with all her might, for fear of losing the great Big Bass.

As she began to haul in her catch the golden rocker began to show above the water. The Woman could not distinguish it rightly by moonlight, but thought: "It is the golden fin of the Bass."

Next came up the child with the golden apple. Again the Woman thought: "It is the golden apple on the fish's fin." And when at last Plunk's head came up, the Woman cried out joyfully: "And here is the head of the great Big Bass."

And as she cried out she hauled in her catch, and when she had hauled it close alongside—why, dearie mine, how am I to tell you rightly how overjoyed were those three when they met again in the boat, all in the moonlight, in the middle of the Unknown Sea?

But they dare not lose any time. They had to pass through the three caverns ere the monstrous watchers should awaken. So they took out the oars and rowed with all their might and main.

But oh dear! the bad luck they had! When the little King awoke and saw his mummy, he remembered her at once. He threw both his little arms round his mummy's neck—and the golden apple fell out of his hand. Down fell the apple into the sea, down to the very bottom and into the Sea King's Castle, and hit the Sea King right on his shoulder!

The Sea King woke up, and bellowed with rage. All the court jumped to their feet. They saw at once that the little King and his servant were missing!

They gave chase. The mermaids swam out under the moonlight; the light foam fairies flew out over the water; runners were sent out to rouse the watchers in the caverns.

But the boat had already passed through the caverns, and so they had to pursue it farther on. Plunk and the Woman were rowing—rowing for dear life, their pursuers close in their wake. The mermaids whipped up the waters; the swift foam fairies darted after the boat; the angry waves rose up in wrath behind them; the wind howled from the clouds. Nearer and nearer came the pursuers. The finest ship afloat would not have had a chance, and how could a tiny two-oared boat? For hours and hours the boat flew on before the tempest, and just as the day began to break, lo, terror gathered from all sides around the boat.

37

For the hurricane beat upon the boat; the crested billows towered above it; the mermaids joined in a ring around it. The ring heaved and swayed around the boat; the mermaids raised their linked hands high to let the mountainous waves pass through, but never let the little craft escape the waves. Sea and storm whistled and roared.

The fear of death was upon Plunk, and in his dire need he cried out:

"Oh, fair Dawn-Maiden, help!"

The Dawn-Maiden arose from the sea. She saw Plunk, but never looked at him. She looked at the little King, but no gift had she for him; but to the faithful Wife she swiftly gave her gift—a broidered kerchief and a pin.

Quickly they hoisted the kerchief, and it became a white sail, and the pin turned into a rudder. The wind filled the sail, so that it bulged like a ripe apple, and the Woman gripped the rudder with a strong hand. The mermaids' ring round the boat was broken; the boat rode upon the azure sea like a star across the blue heavens! A wonder of wonders, it flew over the sea before its terrible pursuers; the fiercer the pursuit, the greater help it was to them; for the swifter the wind blew, the more swiftly yet flew the boat before the wind, and the swifter the sea, the more swiftly rode the boat upon the sea.

Already the rock-bound shore loomed afar, and upon the shore Plunk's little cottage and the bar of white sand before it.

As soon as the land hove in sight, the pursuit slackened. The foam fairies fear the shore; the mermaids keep away from the coast. Wind and waves stayed on the high seas, and only the boat flew straight ahead to land like a child to its mother's lap.

The boat flew to land over the white sand bar, and struck on a rock. The boat split on the rock. Down went sail and rudder; down went the golden cradle; away flew the Golden-winged Bee; and Plunk and his wife and child were left alone on the beach outside their cottage.

When they sat down that night to their supper of wild spinach, they had clean forgotten all that had happened. And but for those twin pipes, there's not a soul would remember it now. But whoever starts to play on the pipes, the fat pipe at once begins to drone out about Plunk:

Harum-scarum Plunk would go
Where the pearls and corals grow;
There he found but grief and woe.

And then the little pipe reminds us of the Woman:

Rise, O Dawn, in loveliness!
Here is new-born happiness;
Were it three times drown'd in ill.
Faith and Love would save it still!

And that is the twin pipes' message to the wide, wide world.

Reygoch

ONCE upon a beautiful summer night the men were watching their horses in the meadow. And as they watched, they fell asleep. And as they slept, the fairies flew out of the clouds to have some sport with the horses, as is the fairies' way. Each fairy caught a horse, mounted it, and then whipped it with her golden hair, urging it round and round the dewy meadow.

Among the fairies there was one quite young and tiny, called Curlylocks, who had come down to earth from the clouds for the first time that night.

Curlylocks thought it lovely to ride through the night like a whirlwind. And it so happened that she had got hold of the most spirited horse of all—a Black—small, but fierce as fire. The Black galloped round and round with the other horses, but he was the swiftest of all. Soon he was all in a lather of foam.

But Curlylocks wanted to ride faster still. She bent down and pinched the Black's right ear. The horse started, reared, and then bolted straight ahead, leaving behind the rest of the horses, the meadow and all, as he flew away like the wind with Curlylocks into the wide, wide world.

Curlylocks thoroughly enjoyed her lightning ride. The Black went like the wind, by field and by river, by meadow and mountain, over dale and hill. "Good gracious! what a lot of things there are in the world!" thought Curlylocks, full of delight as she looked at all the pretty sights. But what pleased her best was when they came through a country where there were mountains all covered with glorious forests, and at the foot of the mountains two golden fields like two great gold kerchiefs, and in the midst of them two white villages, like two white doves, and a little further on a great sheet of water.

But the Black would not stop, neither there nor anywhere, but rushed on and on as if he were possessed.

So the Black carried Curlylocks far and far away till at last they came to a great plain, with a cold wind blowing over it. The Black galloped into the plain, and there was nothing there but yellow sand, neither trees nor grass, and the further they went into that great waste, the colder it grew. But how large that plain is, I cannot tell you, for the good reason that the man does not live who could cross it.

The Black ran on with Curlylocks for seven days and seven nights. The seventh day, just before sunrise, they reached the centre of the plain, and in the centre of the plain they found the ruinous walls of the terribly great city of Frosten, and there it is always bitterly cold.

As the Black raced up to the ancient gates of Frosten, Curlylocks threw her magic veil on the wall, and so caught hold of the wall. The Black galloped away from under her, and so continued his wild career up to his old age to and fro between the huge walls of Frosten, till at last he found the northern gate and galloped out again into the plain—God knows whither!

But Curlylocks came down from the wall and began to walk about the city, and it was cold as cold! Her magic veil, without which she could not fly among the clouds, she wound about her shoulders, for she took great care of it. And so Curlylocks walked and walked about the city of Frosten, and all the time she felt as if she must come upon something very wonderful in this city, which was so marvellous and so great. However, nothing did she see but only great crumbling walls, and nothing did she hear but now and again a stone cracking with the cold.

Suddenly, just as Curlylocks had turned the corner of the very biggest wall, she saw, fast asleep at the foot of the wall, a huge man, bigger than the biggest oak in the biggest forest. The man was dressed in a huge cloak of coarse linen, and the strap he wore for a belt was five fathoms long. His head was as big as the biggest barrel, and his beard was like a shock of corn. He was so big, that man, you might have thought there was a church tower fallen down beside the wall!

This giant was called Reygoch, and he lived at Frosten. All he did was to count the stones of the city of Frosten. He could never have finished counting them but for that huge head of his, as big as a barrel. But he counted and counted—he had counted for a thousand years, and had already counted thirty walls and five gates of the city.

When Curlylocks spied Reygoch, she clasped her hands and wondered. She never thought there could be such an immense creature in the world.

So Curlylocks sat down by Reygoch's ear (and Reygoch's ear was as big as the whole of Curlylocks), and called down his ear:

"Aren't you cold, daddy?"

Reygoch woke up, laughed, and looked at Curlylocks.

"Cold? I should think I was cold," answered Reygoch, and his voice was as deep as distant thunder. Reygoch's big nose was all red with the cold, and his hair and beard were all thick with hoar-frost.

"Dear me!" said Curlylocks, "you're such a big man, and you aren't going to build yourself a roof to keep out the cold?"

"Why should I?" said Reygoch, and laughed again. "The sun will be out presently."

Reygoch heaved himself up so as to sit. He sat up. He clapped his left shoulder with his right hand, and his right shoulder he clapped with the left hand, so as to beat out the hoar-frost; and the hoar-frost came off each shoulder as if it were snow slipping off a roof!

"Look out! look out, daddy! you'll smother me!" cried Curlylocks. But Reygoch could scarcely hear her, because it was a long way from Curlylocks to his ear, so big was he when he sat up.

So Reygoch lifted Curlylocks on to his shoulder, told her his name and his business, and she told him how she had come.

"And here comes the sun," said Reygoch, and pointed for Curlylocks to see.

Curlylocks looked, and there was the sun rising, but so pale and feeble, as if there were no one for him to warm.

"Well, you are a silly, Reygoch!" said Curlylocks—"you are really silly to live here and spend your life counting these tiresome stones of Frosten. Come along, Reygoch, and see how beautiful the world is, and find something more sensible to do."

Now it had never occurred to Reygoch to want a finer home for himself than Frosten city, nor had he ever thought that there might be better work

41

than his in the world. Reygoch always thought, "I was meant to count the stones of Frosten," and had never asked for anything better.

Curlylocks, however, gave him no peace, but persuaded him to come out and see the world with her.

"I'll take you to a lovely country," said Curlylocks, "where there is an ancient forest, and beside the forest two golden fields."

Curlylocks talked for a long time. And old Reygoch had never had anybody to talk to, and so he couldn't resist persuasion.

"Well, let's go!" said he.

Curlylocks was mightily pleased with this.

But now they had to contrive something, so that Reygoch could carry Curlylocks, because Reygoch himself had nothing.

So Curlylocks drew out from her bosom a little bag of pearls. It was her mother who had given Curlylocks these pearls before allowing her to go down to earth, and told her: "If you ever should need anything, just throw down a pearl, and it will turn into whatever you want. Be very careful of those pearls, because there are so many things in the world that you will want more and more as you go on."

Curlylocks took out a tiny seed-pearl, threw it down, and lo, before their eyes there grew a little basket, just as big as Curlylocks, and the basket had a loop attached, just big enough to fit Reygoch's ear.

Curlylocks jumped into the basket; and Reygoch picked up the basket and hung it on his ear like an ear-ring!

Whenever Reygoch laughed, whenever he sneezed or shook his head, Curlylocks rocked as if she were in a swing; and she thought it a capital way of travelling.

So Reygoch started to walk, and had already taken a ten-yard stride, when Curlylocks stopped him, and begged:

"Couldn't we go underground, perhaps, Reygoch dear, so that I might see what there is under the earth?"

"Why not?" answered Reygoch; for he could break into the earth as easy as fun, only it had never entered his head to look what might be underground.

But Curlylocks wanted to know everything about everything, and so they agreed to travel underground until they should arrive under the forest by the golden fields, and there they would come up.

When they had settled that, Reygoch began to break up the earth. He lifted up his great feet and stamped for the first time, and at that the whole of the great city of Frosten shook and a great many walls tumbled down. Reygoch raised his feet a second time and stamped again, and the whole plain quaked. Reygoch raised his feet a third time and stamped, and lo, half the world trembled, the solid earth gaped under Reygoch, and Reygoch and Curlylocks fell into the hole and down under the earth.

When they got there, they found the earth all honeycombed with pillars and passages on every side, and heaven alone knew where they all led to. And they could hear waters rushing and the moaning of the winds.

They followed one of the passages, and for awhile they had light from the hole through which they had fallen. But as they went on it grew darker and darker—black darkness, such as there is nowhere save in the bowels of the earth.

Reygoch tramped calmly on in the dark. With his great hands he felt his way from pillar to pillar.

But Curlylocks was frightened by the great darkness.

She clung to Reygoch's ear and cried: "It's dark, Reygoch dear!"

"Well, and why not?" returned Reygoch. "The dark didn't come to us. It's we have come to it."

Then Curlylocks got cross, because Reygoch never minded anything and she had expected great things from so huge a man.

"I should be in a nice fix with you but for my pearls," said Curlylocks quite angrily.

Then she threw down another pearl, and a tiny lantern grew in her hand, bright as if it were lit with gold. The darkness crept back deeper into the earth, and the light shone far through the underground passages.

Curlylocks was delighted with her lantern, because it showed up all the marvels which had been swallowed by the earth in days of old. In one place she saw lordly castles, with doors and windows all fretted with gold and framed in red marble. In another place were warriors' weapons, slender-barrelled muskets and heavy scimitars studded with gems and precious stones. In a third place she saw long-buried treasures, golden dishes and silver goblets full of gold ducats, and the Emperor's very crown of gold three times refined. All these treasures had been swallowed up by God's will, and it is God's secret why so much treasure should lie there undisturbed.

But Curlylocks was quite dazzled with all these marvels; and instead of going straight ahead by the way they had settled upon, she begged Reygoch to put her down so that she might play about a little and admire all the strange things and gaze upon the wonders of God's secret.

So Reygoch set Curlylocks down, and Curlylocks took her little lantern and ran to the castles, and to the weapons, and to the treasure-hoards. And lest she might lose her little bag of pearls while she was playing, she laid it down beside a pillar.

As for Reygoch, he sat down to rest not far off.

Curlylocks began to play with the treasures; she looked at the beautiful things and rummaged among them. With her tiny hands she scattered the golden ducats, examined the goblets chased in silver, and put upon her head the crown of gold three times refined. She played about, looked round and admired, and at last caught sight of a very slender little ivory staff propped up against a mighty pillar.

But it was just that slender staff that kept the mighty pillar from collapsing, because the pillar was already completely hollowed out by the water. And therefore God had caused that little staff to fall down there, and the staff held up the pillar under the earth.

But Curlylocks wondered:

"Why is that little staff just there?" And she went and picked up the staff to look at it.

But no sooner had Curlylocks taken the staff and moved it than the subterranean passages re-echoed with a terrible rumbling noise. The great pillar trembled, swayed and crashed down amid a whole mountain of falling earth, closing and blocking up the path between Reygoch and Curlylocks. They could neither see nor hear one another, nor could they reach one another....

There was the poor little fairy Curlylocks caught in the bowels of the earth! She was buried alive in that vast grave, and perhaps would never again see

44

those golden fields for which she had set out, and all because she would not go straight on by the way they had intended, but would loiter and turn aside to the right and to the left to pry into God's secrets!

Curlylocks wept and cried, and tried to get to Reygoch. But she found that there was no way through, and that her plight was hopeless; and as for the bag of pearls, which might have helped her, it was buried under the landslide.

When Curlylocks realised this she stopped crying, for she was proud, and she thought: "There is no help for it, and I must die. Reygoch won't come to my rescue, because his wits are too slow even to help himself, let alone to make him remember to help me. So there is nothing for it, and I must die."

So Curlylocks prepared for death. But in case folk should ever find her in her grave she wanted them to know that she came of royal blood. So she set the crown of gold three times refined upon her head, took the ivory staff in her hand, and lay down to die. There was no one beside Curlylocks except her little lantern, burning as if it were lit with gold; and as Curlylocks began to grow cold and stiff, so the lantern burned low and dim.

Reygoch was really an old stupid. When the pillar crashed down and there was the big landslide between him and Curlylocks he never moved, but sat still in the dark. Thus he sat for quite a long time, before it occurred to him to go and find out what had happened.

He felt his way in the dark to the spot where Curlylocks had been, groped about, and realised that the earth had subsided there and that the passage was indeed blocked.

"Eh, but that way is choked up now," considered Reygoch. And nothing else could he think of, but turned round, left the mound of fallen earth and Curlylocks beyond it, and went back by the road they had travelled from Frosten city.

* * * * *

Thus old Reygoch went his way, pillar by pillar. He had already gone a goodish bit; but there was all the time something worrying him. Reygoch himself couldn't imagine what it was that worried him.

He arranged the strap around his waist—perhaps it had been too tight; and then he stretched his arm—perhaps his arm had gone to sleep. Yet it was neither the one nor the other, but something else that worried. Reygoch wondered what in the world it could be. He wondered, and as he wondered he shook his head.

And as Reygoch shook his head, the little basket swung at his ear. And when Reygoch felt how light the basket was, and that there was no Curlylocks inside, a bitter pang shot through his heart and breast, and—simpleton though he was—he knew well enough that he was grieved because he missed Curlylocks, and he realised also that he ought to save her.

It had taken Reygoch a lot of trouble to think out all that; but once he had thought it out, he turned like the wind and flew back to the place where the landslide was, to find Curlylocks behind the heap of earth. He flew, and arrived just in time. Reygoch burrowed away with both hands, and in a little while he had burrowed a big hole, so that he could see Curlylocks lying there, the crown of fine gold on her head. She was already growing cold and rigid, with her little lantern beside her, and the flame of it as feeble as the tiniest little glow-worm.

If Reygoch had cried out in his grief the earth would have rocked, and the little lantern would have gone out altogether—even the little glow-worm light by the side of Curlylocks would have died away.

But Reygoch's throat was all tight with pain, so that he could not cry out. He put out his great big hand and gently picked up poor Curlylocks, who was already quite cold, and warmed her between the hollowed palms of his huge hands as you would warm a starved dicky-bird in winter. And lo! in a little while Curlylocks moved her little head, and at once the lantern burned a little brighter; and then Curlylocks moved her arm, and the lantern burned brighter still. At last Curlylocks opened her eyes, and the lantern burned as brightly as if its flame were pure gold!

Then Curlylocks jumped to her feet, caught hold of Reygoch's beard, and they both of them cried for pure joy. Reygoch's tears were as big as pears and Curlylocks' as tiny as millet-seed, but except for size they were both the same sort; and from that moment these two were mightily fond of one another.

When they had finished their cry, Curlylocks found her pearls, and then they went on. But they touched no more of the things they saw underground, neither the sunken ships with their hoards of treasure, which had worked their way down from the bottom of the sea, nor the red coral, nor the yellow amber which twined round the underground pillars. They touched nothing, but went straight along by the way that would take them to the golden fields.

When they had gone on thus for a long time, Curlylocks asked Reygoch to hold her up; and when he did so, Curlylocks took a handful of earth from above her head.

She took the earth, looked at her hand, and there, among the soil, she found leaves and fibres.

"Here we are, daddy, under the forest beside the golden fields," said Curlylocks. "Let's hurry up and get out."

So Reygoch stretched himself and began to break through the earth with his head.

II

And indeed they were under the forest, just underneath a wooded glen between the two villages and the two counties. No one ever came to this glen but the herd boys and girls from both villages and both counties.

Now there was bitter strife between the two villages—strife over the threshing-floors, and the pastures, and the mills, and the timber-felling, and most of all over the staff of headmanship, which one of the villages had long claimed as belonging to it by rights, and the other would not give up. And so these two villages were at enmity with one another.

But the herd boys and girls of both villages were just simple young folk, who understood nothing about the rights of their elders, and cared less, but met every day on the boundary between the two villages and the two counties. Their flocks mingled and fed together, while the boys played games, and over their games would often be late in bringing the sheep home of an evening.

For this the poor boys and girls would be soundly rated and scolded in both villages. But in one of the villages there was a great-grandfather and a great-grandmother who could remember all that had ever happened in either village, and they said: "Leave the children alone. A better harvest will spring from their childish games than ever from your wheat in the fields."

So the shepherds kept on coming, as before, with their sheep to the glen, and in time the parents stopped bothering about what the children did.

And so it was on the day when Reygoch broke through the earth at that very spot. The boys and girls happened to be all gathered together under the biggest oak, getting ready to go home. One was tying up his shoes, another fixing a thong to a stick, and the girls were collecting the sheep. All of a sudden they heard a dreadful thumping in the earth right underneath their feet! There was a thud, then a second, and at the third thud the earth gaped, and up there came, right in the midst of the shepherds, a fearsome large head as big as a barrel, with a beard like a shock of corn, and the beard still bristling with hoar-frost from Frosten city!

The boys and girls all screamed with fright and fell down in a dead faint—not so much because of the head as big as a barrel, but because of the beard, that looked for all the world like a shock of corn!

So the shepherds fainted away—all but young Lilio, who was the handsomest and cleverest among the lads of both villages and both counties.

Lilio kept his feet, and went close up to see what sort of monster it might be.

"Don't be afraid, children," said Lilio to the shepherds. "The Lord never created that monstrous giant for evil, else he would have killed half the world by now."

So Lilio walked boldly up to Reygoch, and Reygoch lifted the basket with Curlylocks down from his ear and set it on the ground.

"Come—oh come quickly, boys!" cried Lilio. "There is a little girl with him, little and lovely as a star!"

The herd boys and girls got up and began to peep from behind each other at Curlylocks; and those who had at first been the most frightened were now the foremost in coming up to Curlylocks, because, you see, they were always quickest in everything.

No sooner had the herd boys and girls seen dear little Curlylocks than they loved her. They helped her out of her basket, led her to where the turf was softest, and fell to admiring her lovely robes, which were light as gossamer and blue as the sky, and her hair, which was shining and soft as the morning light; but most of all they admired her fairy veil, for she would wave it just for a moment, and then rise from the grass and float in the air.

The herd boys and girls and Curlylocks danced in a ring together, and played all kinds of games. Curlylocks' little feet twinkled for pure joy, her eyes laughed, and so did her lips, because she had found companions who liked the same things as she did.

Then Curlylocks brought out her little bag of pearls to give presents and pleasure to her new friends. She threw down a pearl, and a little tree grew up in their midst, all decked with coloured ribbons, silk kerchiefs and red necklaces for the girls. She threw down a second pearl, and from all parts of the forest came forth haughty peacocks; they stalked and strutted, they flew up and away, shedding their glorious feathers all over the turf, so that the grass fairly sparkled with them. And the herd boys stuck the feathers in their caps and doublets. Yet another pearl did Curlylocks throw out, and from a lofty branch there dropped a golden swing with silken ropes; and when the boys and girls got on the swing, it swooped and stooped as light as a swallow, and as gently as the grand barge of the Duke of Venice.

The children shouted for joy, and Curlylocks threw out all the pearls in her bag one after another, never thinking that she ought to save them; because Curlylocks liked nothing in the world better than lovely games and pretty songs. And so she spent her pearls down to the last little seed pearl, though heaven alone knew how badly she would need them soon, both she and her new friends.

"I shall never leave you any more," cried Curlylocks merrily. And the herd boys and girls clapped their hands and threw up their caps for joy over her words.

Only Lilio had not joined in their games, because he was rather sad and worried that day. He stayed near Reygoch, and from there he watched Curlylocks in all her loveliness, and all the pretty magic she made there in the forest.

Meantime Reygoch had come out of his hole. Out he came and stood up among the trees of the forest, and as he stood there his head rose above the hundred-year-old forest, so terribly big was Reygoch.

Over the forest looked Reygoch, and out into the plain.

The sun had already set, and the sky was all crimson. In the plain you could see the two golden fields spread out like two gold kerchiefs, and in the midst of the fields two villages like two white doves. A little way beyond the two villages flowed the mighty River Banewater, and all along the river rose great grass-grown dykes; and on the dykes you could see herds and their keepers moving.

"Well, well!" said Reygoch, "and to think that I have spent a thousand years in Frosten city, in that desert, when there is so much beauty in the world!" And Reygoch was so delighted with looking into the plain that he just stood

48

there with his great head as big as a barrel turning from right to left, like a huge scarecrow nodding above the tree-tops.

Presently Lilio called to him:

"Sit down, daddy, for fear the elders of the villages should see you."

Reygoch sat down, and the two started talking, and Lilio told Reygoch why he was so sad that day.

"A very wicked thing is going to happen to-day," said Lilio. "I overheard the elders of our village talking last night, and this is what they said: 'Let us pierce the dyke along the River Banewater. The river will widen the hole, the dyke will fall, and the water will flood the enemy village; it will drown men and women, flood the graveyard and the fields, till the water will be level above them, and nothing but a lake to show where the enemy village has been. But our fields are higher, and our village lies on a height, and so no harm will come to us.' And then they really went out with a great ram to pierce the dyke secretly and at dead of night. But, daddy," continued Lilio, "I know that our fields are not so high, and I know that the water will overflow them too, and before the night is over there will be a lake where our two villages used to be. And that is why I am so sad."

They were still talking when a terrible noise and clamour arose from the plain.

"There!" cried Lilio, "the dreadful thing has happened!"

Reygoch drew himself up, picked up Lilio, and the two looked out over the plain. It was a sad sight to see! The dyke was crumbling, and the mighty Black Banewater rolling in two arms across the beautiful fields. One arm rolled towards the one village, and the second arm towards the other village. Animals were drowning, the golden fields disappeared below the flood. Above the graves the crosses were afloat, and both villages rang with cries and shouting. For in both villages the elders had gone out to the threshing-floors with cymbals, drums and fifes, and there they were drumming and piping away each to spite the other village, so crazed were they with malice, while over and above that din the village dogs howled dismally, and the women and children wept and wailed.

"Daddy," cried Lilio, "why have I not your hands to stop the water?"

Terrified and bewildered by the dreadful clamour in the plain, the herd boys and girls crowded round Reygoch and Lilio.

When Curlylocks heard what was the matter she called out quick and sprightly, as befits a little fairy:

"Come on, Reygoch—come on and stop the water!"

"Yes, yes, let's go!" cried the herd boys of both villages and both counties, as they wept and sobbed without stopping. "Come on, Reygoch, and take us along too!"

Reygoch stooped, gathered up Lilio and Curlylocks (who was still carrying her lantern) in his right hand, and all the rest of the herd boys and girls in his left, and then Reygoch raced with ten-fathom strides through the forest clearing and down into the plain. Behind him ran the sheep, bleating with terror. And so they reached the plain.

Through fog and twilight ran Reygoch with the children in his arms and the terrified flocks at his heels in frantic flight—all running towards the dyke. And out to meet them flowed the Black Banewater, killing and drowning as it flowed. It is terribly strong, is that water. Stronger than Reygoch? Who knows? Will it sweep away Reygoch, too? Will it drown those poor herd boys and girls also, and must the dear little Fairy Curlylocks die—and she as lovely as a star?

So Reygoch ran on across the meadow, which was still dry, and came all breathless to the dyke, where there was a great breach, through which the river was pouring with frightful force.

"Stop it up, Reygoch—stop it up!" wailed the boys and girls.

Not far from the dyke there was a little mound in the plain.

"Put us on that mound," cried Curlylocks briskly.

Reygoch set down Lilio and Curlylocks and the herd boys and girls on the hillock, and the sheep and lambs crowded round them. Already the hillock was just an island in the middle of the water.

But Reygoch took one mighty stride into the water and then lay down facing the dyke, stopping up the breach with his enormous chest. For a little while the water ceased to flow; but it was so terribly strong that nothing on earth could stop it. The water pressed forward; it eddied round Reygoch's shoulders; it broke through under him, over him, about him—everywhere— and rolled on again over the plain. Reygoch stretched out both arms and piled up the earth in great handfuls; but as fast as he piled it up, the water carried it away.

And in the plain the water kept on rising higher and higher; fields, villages, cattle, threshing-floors, not one of them could be seen any more. Of both villages, the roofs and church steeples were all that showed above the flood.

Even around the hillock where the herd boys and girls were standing with Lilio and Curlylocks the flood was rising higher and higher. The poor young things were weeping and crying, some for their mothers, others for their brothers and sisters, and some for their homes and gardens; because they saw that both villages had perished, and not a soul saved—and the water rising about them, too!

So they crowded up higher and higher upon the hillock; they huddled together around Lilio and Curlylocks, who were standing side by side in the midst of their friends.

Lilio stood still and white as marble; but Curlylocks' eyes shone, and she held up her lantern towards Reygoch to give him light for his work. Curlylocks' veil rose and fluttered in the night wind and hovered above the water, as though the little fairy were about to fly away and vanish from among all these terrors.

"Curlylocks! Curlylocks! don't go! Don't leave us!" wailed the herd boys, to whom it seemed as if there were an angel with them while they could look upon Curlylocks.

"I'm not going—I'm not going away!" cried Curlylocks. But her veil fluttered, as if it would carry her away of its own accord, over the water and up into the clouds.

Suddenly they heard a scream. The water had risen and caught one of the girls by the hem of her skirt and was washing her away. Lilio stooped just in time, seized the girl, and pulled her back on to the hillock.

"We must tie ourselves together," cried the herd boys; "we must be tied each to the other, or we shall perish."

"Here, children—here!" cried Curlylocks, who had a kind and pitiful heart.

Quickly she stripped her magic veil off her shoulders and gave it to the herd girls. They tore the veil into strips, knotted the strips into long ropes, and bound themselves together, each to other, round Lilio and Curlylocks. And round the shepherds bleated the poor sheep in terror of being drowned.

But Curlylocks was now among these poor castaways, no better off than the rest of them. Her pearls she had wasted on toys, and her magic veil she had given away and torn up out of the goodness of her heart, and now she could no longer fly, nor save herself out of this misery.

But Lilio loved Curlylocks better than anything else in the world, and when the water was already up to his feet he called:

"Don't be afraid, Curlylocks! I will save you and hold you up!" And he held up Curlylocks in his arms.

With one hand Curlylocks clung round Lilio's neck, and with the other she held up her little lantern aloft towards Reygoch.

And Reygoch, lying on his chest in the water, was all the time steadily fighting the flood. Right and left of Reygoch rose the ruins of the dyke like two great horns. Reygoch's beard was touzled, his shoulders were bleeding. Yet he could not stop the Banewater, and the flood round the hillock was rising and rising to drown the poor remnant there. And now it was night—yea, midnight.

All of a sudden a thought flashed through Curlylocks, and through all the sobbing and crying she laughed aloud as she called to Reygoch:

"Reygoch, you old simpleton! why don't you *sit* between these two horns of the dyke? Why don't you dam the flood with your shoulders?"

The herd boys and girls stopped wailing at once. So dumbfounded were they at the idea that not one of them had thought of that before!

"Uhuhu!" was all you could hear, and that was Reygoch laughing. And when Reygoch laughs, mind you, it's no joke! All the water round him boiled and bubbled as he shook with laughter over his own stupidity!

Then Reygoch stood up, faced about, and—in a twinkling—he sat down between those two horns!

And then happened the most wonderful thing of all! For the Black Banewater stood as though you had rolled a wall into the breach! It stood, and could not rise above Reygoch's shoulders, but followed its usual course, as before, the whole current behind Reygoch's back. And surely that was a most marvellous rescue!

The boys and girls were saved from the worst of the danger; and Reygoch, sitting comfortably, took up earth in handfuls and all slow-and-surely rebuilt the dyke under himself and on either hand. He began in the middle of the night, and when the dawn broke, the job was finished. And just as the sun rose, Reygoch got up from the dyke with his work done, and started combing his beard, which was all caked with mud, twigs, and little fishes.

But the poor boys and girls were not yet done with their troubles; for where were they to go, and how were they to get there? There they stood on the top of the hillock. All around them was a waste of water. Nothing was to be seen of the two villages but just a few roofs—and not a soul alive in either. To be sure, the villagers might have saved themselves if they had taken refuge in their attics. But in both villages everybody had gone to the threshing-floor with cymbals and fifes to make merry, so that each could watch the destruction of the other. And when the water was up to their waists, they were still clanging their cymbals; and when it was up to their necks, they still blew their fifes for gratified spite. And so they were drowned, one and all, with their fifes and cymbals—and serve them right for their malice and uncharitableness!

So the poor children were left without a soul to cherish or protect them, all houseless and homeless.

"We're not sparrows, to live on the housetops," said the boys sadly, as they saw only the roofs sticking out of the water, "and we're not foxes, to live in burrows in the hills. If someone could clear our villages of the water, we might make shift to get along somehow, but as it is, we might as well jump into the water with our flocks and be drowned like the rest, for we have nowhere and no one to turn to."

That was a sad plight indeed, and Reygoch himself was dreadfully sorry for them. But here was an evil he could in no wise remedy. He looked out over the water and said: "There's too much water here for me to bale out or to drink up so as to clear your villages. Eh, children, what shall I do for you?"

But then up and spoke Lilio, that was the wisest lad in these parts:

"Reygoch, daddy, if *you* cannot drink so much water, *the Earth can.* Break a hole in the ground, daddy, and drain off the water into the earth."

Dearie me! and wasn't that great wisdom in a lad no bigger than Reygoch's finger?

Forthwith Reygoch stamped on the ground and broke a hole; and the Earth, like a thirsty dragon, began to drink and to drink, and swallow, and suck down into herself all that mighty water from off the whole plain. Before long the Earth had gulped down all the water; villages, fields, and meadows reappeared, ravaged and mud-covered, to be sure, but with everything in its right place.

The young castaways cheered up at the sight, but none was so glad as Curlylocks. She clapped her hands and cried:

"Oh, won't it be lovely when the fields all grow golden again and the meadows green!"

But hereupon the herd boys and girls were all downcast once more, and Lilio said:

"Who will show us how to till the ground now that not one of our parents is left alive?"

And indeed, far and wide, there was not a soul alive older than that company of helpless young things in the midst of the ravaged plain, and none with them but Reygoch, who was so big and clumsy and simple that he could not turn his head inside one of their houses, nor did he know anything about ploughing or husbandry.

So they were all in the dumps once more, and most of all Reygoch, who was so fond of pretty Curlylocks, and now he could do nothing for her nor her friends!

And, worst of all, Reygoch was getting horribly homesick for his desolate city of Frosten. This night he had swallowed mud enough to last him a thousand years, and seen more than enough of trouble. And so he was just dying to be back in his vast, empty city, where he had counted the stones in peace for so many hundred years.

So the herd boys were very crestfallen, and Lilio was crestfallen, and Reygoch the most crestfallen of all. And really it was sad to look upon all these poor boys and girls, doomed to perish without their parents and wither like a flower cut off from its root.

Only Curlylocks looked gaily about her, right and left, for nothing could damp her good spirits.

Suddenly Curlylocks cried out:

"Look—oh look! What are those people? Oh dear, but they must have seen sights and wonders!"

All looked towards the village, and there, at one of the windows, appeared the heads of an aged couple—an old man and an old woman. They waved their kerchiefs, they called the young people by name, and laughed till their wrinkled faces all shone with joy. They were great-grandfather and great-grandmother, who had been the only sensible people in the two villages, and had saved themselves by taking refuge in the attic!

Oh dear! If the children had seen the sun at his rising and the morning star at that attic window, they would not have shouted so for joy. The very heavens rang again as they called out:

"Granny! Grandad!"

They raced to the village like young whippets, Curlylocks in front, with her golden hair streaming in the wind, and after them the ewes and lambs. They never stopped till they reached the village, and there grandfather and grandmother were waiting for them at the gate. They welcomed them, hugged them, and none of them could find words to thank God enough for

His mercy in giving grandad and grandma so much wisdom as to make them take refuge in the attic! And that was really a very good thing, because these were only quite simple villages, where there were no books nor written records; and who would have reminded the herd boys and girls of the consequences of wickedness if grandad and grandma had not been spared?

When they had done hugging each other, they remembered Reygoch. They looked round the plain, but there was no Reygoch. He was gone—gone all of a sudden, the dear huge thing—gone like a mouse down its hole.

And Reygoch had indeed gone like a mouse down its hole. For when grandpa and grandma appeared at the attic window, Reygoch got a fright such as he had never yet had in his life. He was terrified at the sight of their furrowed, wrinkled, withered old faces.

"Oh dear! oh dear! what a lot of trouble these old people must have been through in these parts to have come to look like that!" thought Reygoch; and in his terror he that very instant jumped down into the hole through which the Black Banewater had sunk down, and so ran away back to his desolate Frosten city.

* * * * *

All went well in the village. Grandad and Grandma taught the young folk, and the young folk ploughed and sowed. Upon the grandparents' advice they built just one village, one threshing-floor, one church, and one graveyard, so that there should be no more jealousy nor trouble.

All went well; but the best of all was that in the heart of the village stood a beautiful tower of mountain marble, and on the top of it they had made a garden, where blossomed oranges and wild olive. There lived Curlylocks, the lovely fairy, and looked down upon the land that had been so dear to her from the moment when she first came to earth.

And of an evening, when the field work was done, Lilio would lead the herd boys and girls to the tower, and they would sing songs and dance in a ring in the garden with Curlylocks, always lovely, gentle, and joyous.

But under the earth Reygoch once more fell in with the Black Banewater as it roared and burbled underneath, while he wrestled with it till he forced it deeper and deeper into the earth, and right down to the bottom of the Pit, so that it might never again serve the spite and envy of man. And then Reygoch went on to Frosten city. There he is sitting to this very day, counting the stones and praying the Lord never again to tempt him away from that vast and desolate spot, which is the very place for one so big and so simple.

Bridesman Sun and Bride Bridekins

ONCE upon a time there was a miller and his wife, and both were miserly and hard of heart. When the Emperor's servants brought corn to be ground, the miller would grind the corn free of all charge and send the Emperor a gift into the bargain, only to gain favour with the mighty Emperor and his daughter, the proud princess. But when poor folk came to have their corn ground, the miller would take one measure in payment for every two that he ground, and without that he would not grind at all.

One day, just about Yuletide and in the time of bitter frost, an old wife came to the mill—an old wife all patches and tatters. The mill stood in a little grove by the stream, and no one could say whence that old wife had come.

But this wasn't just an old wife like other old wives; it was Mother Muggish. Now Muggish could turn herself into any mortal thing, a bird or a snake, or an old woman or a young girl. And besides that she could do anything, both good and bad. But woe to him who got into her bad books, for she was very spiteful. Muggish lived in the morass on the fringe of the bog where the autumn sun dwelt. And with her the sun put up over the long winter night; for Muggish knew potent herbs and powerful spells; she would nurse and cherish the feeble old sun till he grew young again at Yuletide and started on his way once more.

"Good day to you," Mother Muggish called out to the miller and his wife. "Just grind this bag of corn for me."

The old wife stood the bag on the floor, and the miller agreed:

"I'll grind it for you; half the bag for you for your cake, and half for me for my trouble."

"Not so, my son! I shall not have enough for my Yuletide cake, because I have six sons, and for seventh my grandson, the Sun, who was born to-day."

"Go away and don't talk rubbish, you old fool!" burst out the miller. "A likely one you are to be the Sun's grandmother!"

So they argued this way and that; but the miller wouldn't consent to grind for less than one-half the bag, and so the old wife picked up her bag again and went away by the way she came.

But the miller had a daughter, a beautiful girl, called Bride Bridekins. When she was born, the fairies bathed her in the water that falls from the wheel, so that all evils should turn from her, even as water runs away from a mill. And, moreover, the fairies foretold that at her wedding the Sun should be bridesman. Just fancy! she was the Sun's little bride! So they called her Bride Bridekins, and she was most beautiful and smiling as a summer's day.

Bride Bridekins was sorry when the miller sent away the old wife so unkindly. She went out and waited in the wood for the old wife, and said:

"Come again to-morrow, Mother, when I shall be alone. I will grind your corn for you for nothing."

Next day the miller and his wife went into the wood to cut the Yule log, and Bride Bridekins was left alone.

Before long the old wife came up with her bag.

"Good fortune be yours, young maiden," said the wife.

"And yours, too," returned Bride Bridekins. "Wait a moment, Mother, till we open the mill."

The mill was worked by a little wheel which caught the water with four paddles set cross-wise, which turned like a spindle. Now the miller had shut off the water, and Bride Bridekins had to wade up to her knees in the icy stream to open the sluice.

The mill clattered, round went the mill-stones, and Bride Bridekins ground the old wife's corn. She filled up the bag with flour and took nothing for her pains.

"Eh, thank you kindly, maiden," said Mother Muggish, "and I'll help you whithersoever your feet may carry you, since your feet you did not save from the ice-cold wave, nor grudge your hands to soil with unrequited toil. And, moreover, I'll tell my grandson, the Sun, to whom he owes his Yuletide cake." And the old wife took up her bag and went.

From that day nothing would prosper in the mill without Bride Bridekins. Unless her hand was on the mill, the paddles would not take the water; unless she looked in the bin, there would be no flour in it. No matter how much might fall into it from the grain-box, it was all lost on the floor; the bin remained empty unless Bride Bridekins fed the mill. And so it was with everything in and about the mill.

This went on for many a day, on and on and never any change, till the miller and his wife began to be jealous of their daughter and to hate her. The harder the girl worked and the more she earned, the blacker they looked at her, because it came to her as easy as a song, and to them not even with toiling and moiling.

It was upon a morning about Beltane time, when the Sun, strong and flaming, travels across one-half of heaven like a ball of pure gold. The Sun no longer slept in the morass, nor did Muggish foster him now; but the Sun was lord of the world, and sky and earth obeyed him. Bride Bridekins sat at Beltane time beside the mill and thought to herself:

"If I could only get away, since I cannot please these cross-patches anyhow!"

And just as she thought this, there appeared before her the old wife, who was really Muggish.

"I will help you, but you must obey me in all things, and take care not to offend me," said the old wife. "This very morning the proud princess walked in the meadow and lost the keys of her chest and her wardrobe, and now she cannot get at her crown nor her robes either. So the princess has caused it to be proclaimed that whoever finds the keys, if it be a youth the princess will become his true love and bride-to-be, and if it be a maiden, the princess will take her for her first lady-in-waiting. So you come away with me, and I will

56

show you where the keys are lying among the love-lies-bleeding that grows in the meadow. You will bring the princess her keys and become her first lady-in-waiting. You will be dressed in silk and sit by the princess's knee."

Then Muggish at once turned herself into a quail, and Bride Bridekins followed her.

So they came to the meadow in front of the Emperor's castle. Gallant knights and noble dames walked about the meadow, and around the meadow stood their esquires holding mettlesome steeds. One steed only was not held by a squire, but by a barefoot boy. This horse belonged to Oleg the Warden, and it was the most fiery steed of all. And Oleg the Warden himself was the most excellent knight under the sun. You might know Oleg the Warden amid ever so many earls and nobles, because his attire was plain and without ornament, but his white plume, the prize of valour, distinguished him above all the rest.

So the knights and dames walked about the meadow, all trampling the grass with their shoes in their anxiety to find the keys. Only Oleg the Warden kept but a poor look-out for the keys, taking the matter as a mere jest and idle pastime. But from her window the Emperor's daughter looked out and watched to see whom fortune would favour. Very careful watch did she keep, the proud princess, and repeated spells for luck so that Oleg the Warden should find the keys.

When Bride Bridekins came with the quail running before her, not a soul in the meadow noticed her but only Oleg the Warden.

"Never yet have I seen so sweet a maiden," thought Oleg the Warden, and strode towards her.

But just then the Emperor's daughter also noticed Bride Bridekins from her window, and so proud and heartless was she that she never stopped to look how sweet the maiden was, but grew very angry, and said: "A fine plight should I be in were that common wench there to find the keys and become my lady-in-waiting!" Thus thinking, she at once sent out her servants to drive away the girl.

Bride Bridekins went over the meadow where-ever the quail led her. They came to the middle of the meadow, where the love-lies-bleeding grew tall. The quail parted two leaves at the foot of a tuft of love-lies-bleeding, and under them lay the keys.

Bride Bridekins bent down and picked up the keys; but when she looked up to the Emperor's castle and saw the proud princess, Bride Bridekins became frightened, and thought: "How should I become the princess's lady-in-waiting?"

As she thought this she looked up, and lo, beside her stood a glorious knight, as he might have been sworn brother to the Sun. And that was Oleg the Warden.

Quickly Bride Bridekins made up her mind to disobey Muggish's commands, and she held out the keys to Oleg the Warden.

"Take the keys, unknown knight, and let the Emperor's daughter be your true love and bride-to-be," said Bride Bridekins, and could not take her eyes off the glorious knight.

But at that moment came the servants with whips, and roughly rated Bride Bridekins so as to drive her away from the meadow, according to the princess's commands. When Oleg the Warden saw this, he was soon resolved, and thus did he answer Bride Bridekins:

"Thank you for the keys, sweet maiden; but I have made up my mind otherwise. *You* shall be my true love and bride-to-be, because you are fairer than the morning star. Here is my good horse; he will carry us to my Barren Marches."

Gladly did Bride Bridekins go with Oleg the Warden, and he lifted her beside him on to his horse. As the good steed carried them swiftly past the Emperor's daughter sitting at her window. Oleg the Warden threw her the keys so skilfully that they caught right on the window latch!

"There are your keys, august Princess!" cried Oleg the Warden. "Wear your crown and your robes in all happiness, for I have taken the maiden for myself."

All that night Oleg the Warden rode on with Bride Bridekins, and at dawn they arrived in the Barren Marches, at the oaken stronghold of Oleg the Warden. Round the stockade there were three moats, and in the midst of the stockade stood a smoke-blacked house.

"Behold the Castle of Oleg the Warden!" said the knight to Bride Bridekins, and he laughed himself because his castle was not more splendid. But Bride Bridekins laughed still more heartily because she was to be the lady of such a glorious knight.

So they settled at once upon the wedding guests, so as to celebrate the marriage. They invited twenty gallants and twenty orphan maids, because that was all the people there were in the Barren Marches. And so that they might be more and merrier, they also asked the Wild Wolf and his Mate from the hills, and the Tawny Eagle, and the Grey Goshawk; and Bride Bridekins asked two bridesmaids—the Turtle Dove and the Slender Swallow.

And Bride Bridekins even boasted to Oleg the Warden:

"If the Sun were to recognise me, he too would come to the wedding. The Sun would have been bridesman at the wedding, for so did the fairies foretell."

And so the wedding guests assembled in the soot-blacked castle, to make merry—and never knew of the ill fate in store for them.

* * * * *

Now it had stung the proud princess to the heart when Oleg the Warden had flung her the keys, and before so many nobles, before earls and knights, refused the august princess and preferred a nameless maiden.

So the princess persuaded the Emperor, her father, and begged and entreated him till he lent her his mighty army. Well mounted, the army advanced upon the Barren Marches of Oleg the Warden with the wrathful princess at its head.

The guests were just at table when the army came in sight. It was so great that it covered all the Barren Marches till you could not see so much as a patch of earth for it. And in front of the army a herald cried aloud for all the world to hear:

Behold a gallant army
 Has taken the field;
The Warden is a rebel,
 We bid him to yield.
Alive shall he be taken
 That freedom loved best;
But the heart shall be riven
 From his lady's breast.

When Oleg the Warden heard this, he asked Bride Bridekins: "Are you afraid, lovely maiden?"

"I am not afraid," she smilingly made answer. "I put my trust in the Grey Wolf and his Mate, in your twenty gallants and twenty orphans, and most of all in the knight Oleg the Warden. And besides that I have two brave brides-maids—the Turtle Dove and the Slender Swallow."

Oleg the Warden smiled, and already the wedding guests had lightly sprung to their feet. They seized their warriors' weapons, both gallants and orphans, and stood by the windows of the soot-blacked castle stringing their good bows with silken cords as they waited for the princess and her army. But that army was so mighty that neither Oleg the Warden, nor his wedding guests, nor the soot-blacked house were able to withstand it.

The first to fall were the Grey Wolf and his Mate; for they jumped the stockade and the moats and rushed straight at the Emperor's army to tear out the proud princess's eyes in the midst of her army. But a hundred maces rose in the air; the soldiers defended the proud princess, the Eagle and the Grey Goshawk had their pinions broken, and then the heavy horses trampled them into the black earth.

The great host came nearer and nearer to the soot-blacked house. When it was fairly on the threshold the wedding guests loosed their silken bow-strings and greeted the soldiers with a shower of arrows.

But the wrathful archers of the wrathful princess did not stop!

Arrows flew hither and thither. There were archers past counting in the army, so that their arrows flew in at the windows of the soot-blacked house like a plague from heaven. Each gallant had his two or three wounds to show, and each orphan some ten.

But the most grievous wound of all was upon Oleg the Warden. His good right hand hung powerless, so greatly was he overcome by his wound.

Quickly Bride Bridekins stepped up to Oleg the Warden to wash his wound in the courtyard of the soot-blacked house. While she was washing his wound, Oleg the Warden said to her: "It's a poor fortune we have garnered, my Bride Bridekins. There are none left for you to put your trust in, and here is the host at the gates of the soot-blacked house. They will break down the oak stockade, batter down the ancient gates. We are lost; this is the end of us—wolves and eagles, and gallants and orphans, and Oleg the Warden and his Bride Bridekins!"

But Bride Bridekins considered sadly, and then she said:

"Do not fear, brave Warden. I will send the Turtle Dove to fetch Muggish from her morass. There is nothing Muggish does not know and nothing she cannot do, and she will help us."

So Bride Bridekins sent out the swift Turtle Dove. Away flew the grey dove swifter than an arrow from the string, nor did the soldiers' darts overtake her. Off she flew and brought back Muggish from the bog. But Muggish had turned herself into a raven and perched upon the gable of the soot-blacked House.

Already the soldiers were battering at the entrance. Heavy clubs hammered on the doors and portals, banging and clanging till all the courts and passages of the soot-blacked house rang again, as though a host from the nethermost Pit were beating on the gates of Oleg the Warden.

"Fair greeting, dear Muggish!" the lovely Bride appealed to the black raven—"fair greeting! Help us against the Princess's malice, or else we must all die untimely!"

But Muggish had only bided her time spitefully for an opportunity to give vent to her grievance. Flapping her black wings, the raven said:

"Save yourself, my little dove! If you had listened to me, you would have given the Princess her keys. You would have basked in royal grace, beside the Princess had your place, in sumptuous silk fair to behold, sipping wine from a cup of gold. But now you have gotten your heart's desire. Here you are in the soot-blacked house with none but sore-wounded beggars within and a countless host outside. Seek help from those whose counsel brought you to this!"

When Oleg the Warden heard this, he sprang to his feet, all wounded as he was, and wrathfully cried out:

"Leave this unprofitable business, Bride Bridekins! When had a hero help from a raven? And you," he called to Muggish, "get off my roof, you black bird of ill-omen, lest I waste a good swift arrow and shoot the bird upon my gable!" With that Oleg the Warden embraced Bride Bridekins and said:

"When I perish in the midst of the Emperor's host, go, my lovely little Bride! submit yourself to the Princess, and you shall be lady-in-waiting to the proud Princess, who should have been true love and lady of Oleg the Warden." For a moment Oleg the Warden flinched; but then he tore himself away from his bride, and rushed through the courtyard and passage to raise the oaken bars, to throw open the gates to the countless host, to perish or cut his way through their numbers.

Bride Bridekins was left alone in the castle, and above her on the roof perched the black raven. She could hear the heavy oaken bars falling; now the ancient gates must yield; another moment and the cruel soldiers will burst in, take Oleg prisoner, and rive the heart out of the breast of her, sweet child! Bride Bridekins' thoughts chased through her brain: What is to be done, and how?

The lovely bride looked all around to see if there were any found to pity her in her distress. She bent her beauteous eyes to earth, and raised them heavenward. As she raised them heavenward the Sun travelled across the zenith in a blaze of pure gold. And as she looked at the Sun, the Sun marvelled at so much loveliness, and at once looked back at her. The Sun and Bride Bridekins looked at one another, and as they looked, they recognised one another, and at once the Sun remembered. "Why, that is the little bride whose Bridesman the Sun was to be! In a lucky hour she gave me my Yuletide bread, and in a yet luckier moment she sought me overhead."

Just one moment before the Sun had heard Muggish mocking Bride Bridekins and spitefully refusing to help her. So now the Sun thundered forth his anger. All the land fell silent with fear; axes and clubs were dropped in terror as the Sun thundered at Muggish:

"Eh, foster-mother, heart of stone! were the world's justice to be carved by spite, what crooked justice would pervert the right! If thou from slime hast reared me, yet content art thou to keep the slime thine element! With me thou hast not strode across the sky, nor from the heavens downward bent thine eye to learn how justice should be born of light. Fie, foster-mother, heart of stone! What! should the Sun at Beltane in his might forget who sent him gifts on Yule night, when he was a feeble babe? Or shall Bridesman Sun take it ill of the bride that she left the Emperor's palace and the Princess's court because she preferred a hero in her heart? Down with you into the earth, black-hearted nurse! so that you underground, and I from the skies, may help yon worthy knight and his lovely lady."

Sky and earth obey the Sun, and how should the black raven—and that was Muggish—withstand his commands? Upon the instant Muggish sank into the earth to do the Sun's bidding.

And strong as the Sun had been before, he now made himself yet stronger. The Sun smote from above; he scorched the Barren Marches; he seared heaven and earth; he would have melted the Mountain of Brass!

Upon the cruel soldiers' heads their helmets dissolved; their heavy armour melted; spears and axes grew red-hot. Heat overcame the wrathful princess; heat overcame the multitude of archers as their brains grilled inside their helmets, and their breasts laboured with the heat under their armour. Who had not the shelter of a roof could not live. All the host was struck down by the heat. They fell one atop of the other. A man would call upon his sworn brother, and then the voice would cease as the speaker perished.

While the Sun was thus smiting the cruel soldiers, Muggish helped the Sun from underground. She opened deep bogholes under their feet. Whenever the Sun struck down a man, there a boghole would gape beneath him. He slipped into the bog, and the bog closed above him; where a man stood, there his grave yawned for him.

So the soldiers vanished one by one, and the archers one by one, and the weapons of war, and the clubs and the axes. It was terrible to behold such a vast army stricken by the judgment of the Sun from the skies. The Sun was executioner and the earth gravedigger. Yet a little while, an hour or two, and the great host had vanished—not a soul was left alive in the Barren Marches. Only those who were under the roof of the soot-blacked house, they were left alive.

Once more all was still in the Barren Marches; and now the lovely lady. Bride Bridekins, peeped joyously from her window to watch her bridesman grow mild, now that he had done with slaying spite upon the earth.

Soon the wounds healed upon the gallants, for they had good luck to help them; and the orphans recovered still more quickly, because hardship is a good school. As for Oleg Ban, he could not pine with such a true love as Bride Bridekins beside him. Early in the morning the Slender Swallow flew out with a greeting for the Sun. At nightfall the Swallow returned with greetings from the Sun, bidding them prepare the wedding feast for the morrow, for he would come to give away the bride.

So they made ready, and it all fell out as they had planned. And such a wedding as they had, and such songs as were sung that day in the Barren Marches you'll not find again in a hundred years, nor throughout nine empires.

Stribor's Forest

ONE day a young man went into Stribor's Forest and did not know that the Forest was enchanted and that all manner of magic abode there. Some of its magic was good and some was bad—to each one according to his deserts.

Now this Forest was to remain enchanted until it should be entered by someone who preferred his sorrows to all the joys of this world.

The young man set to and cut wood, and presently sat down on a stump to rest, for it was a fine winter's day. And out of the stump slipped a snake, and began to fawn upon him. Now this wasn't a real snake, but a human being transformed into a snake for its sins, and it could only be set free by one who was willing to wed it. The snake sparkled like silver in the sun as it looked up into the young man's eyes.

"Dear me, what a pretty snake! I should rather like to take it home," said the young man in fun.

"Here's the silly fool who is going to help me out of my trouble," thought the sinful soul within the snake. So she made haste and turned herself at once out of a snake into a most beautiful woman standing there before the young man. Her sleeves were white and embroidered like butterflies' wings, and her feet were tiny like a countess's. But because her thoughts had been evil, the tongue in her mouth remained a serpent's tongue.

"Here I am! Take me home and marry me!" said the snake-woman to the youth.

Now if this youth had only had presence of mind and remembered quickly to brandish his hatchet at her and call out: "I certainly never thought of wedding a piece of forest magic," why, then the woman would at once have turned again into a snake, wriggled back into the stump, and no harm done to anybody.

But he was one of your good-natured, timid and shy youths; moreover, he was ashamed to say "No" to her, when she had transformed herself all on his account. Besides, he liked her because she was pretty, and he couldn't know in his innocence what had remained inside her mouth.

So he took the Woman by the hand and led her home. Now that youth lived with his old Mother, and he cherished his Mother as though she were the image of a saint.

"This is your daughter-in-law," said the youth, as he entered the house with the Woman.

"The Lord be thanked, my son," replied his Mother, and looked at the pretty girl. But the Mother was old and wise, and knew at once what was inside her daughter-in-law's mouth.

The daughter-in-law went out to change her dress, and the Mother said to her son:

"You have chosen a very pretty bride, my boy; only beware, lest she be a snake."

The youth was dumbfounded with astonishment. How could his Mother know that the other had been a snake? And his heart grew angry within him as he thought: "Surely my Mother is a witch." And from that moment he hated his Mother.

So the three began to live together, but badly and discordantly. The daughter-in-law was ill-tempered, spiteful, greedy and proud.

Now there was a mountain peak there as high as the clouds, and one day the daughter-in-law bade the old Mother go up and fetch her snow from the summit for her to wash in.

"There is no path up there," said the Mother.

"Take the goat and let her guide you. Where she can go up, there you can tumble down," said the daughter-in-law.

The son was there at the time, but he only laughed at the words, simply to please his wife.

This so grieved the Mother that she set out at once for the peak to fetch the snow, because she was tired of life. As she went her way she thought to ask God to help her; but she changed her mind and said: "For then God would know that my son is undutiful."

65

But God gave her help all the same, so that she safely brought the snow back to her daughter-in-law from the cloud-capped peak.

Next day the daughter-in-law gave her a fresh order:

"Go out on to the frozen lake. In the middle of the lake there is a hole. Catch me a carp there for dinner."

"The ice will give way under me, and I shall perish in the lake," replied the old Mother.

"The carp will be pleased if you go down with him," said the daughter-in-law.

And again the son laughed, and the Mother was so grieved that she went out at once to the lake. The ice cracked under the old woman, and she wept so that the tears froze on her face. But yet she would not pray to God for help; she would keep it from God that her son was sinful.

"It is better that I should perish," thought the Mother as she walked over the ice.

But her time had not yet come. And therefore a gull flew over her head, bearing a fish in its beak. The fish wriggled out of the gull's beak and fell right at the feet of the old woman. The Mother picked up the fish and brought it safely to her daughter-in-law.

On the third day the Mother sat by the fire, and took up her son's shirt to mend it. When her daughter-in-law saw that, she flew at her, snatched the shirt out of her hands, and screamed:

"Stop that, you blind old fool! That is none of your business."

And she would not let the Mother mend her son's shirt.

Then the old woman's heart was altogether saddened, so that she went outside, sat in that bitter cold on the bench before the house, and cried to God:

"Oh God, help me!"

At that moment she saw a poor girl coming towards her. The girl's bodice was all torn and her shoulder blue with the cold, because the sleeve had given way. But still the girl smiled, for she was bright and sweet-tempered. Under her arm she carried a bundle of kindling-wood.

"Will you buy wood for kindling, Mother?" asked the girl.

"I have no money, my dear; but if you like I will mend your sleeve," sadly returned the old Mother, who was still holding the needle and thread with which she had wanted to mend her son's shirt.

So the old Mother mended the girl's sleeve, and the girl gave her a bundle of kindling-wood, thanked her kindly, and went on happy because her shoulder was no longer cold.

II

That evening the daughter-in-law said to the Mother:

"We are going out to supper with godmother. Mind you have hot water for me when I come back."

The daughter-in-law was greedy and always on the look-out to get invited for a meal.

So the others went out, and the old woman was left alone. She took out the kindling-wood which the poor girl had given her, lit the fire on the hearth, and went into the shed for wood.

As she was in the shed fetching the wood, she suddenly heard something in the kitchen a-bustling and a-rustling—"hist, hist!"

"Whoever is that?" called the old Mother from the shed.

"Brownies! Brownies!" came the answer from the kitchen in voices so tiny, for all the world like sparrows chirping under the roof.

The old woman wondered what on earth was going on there in the dark, and went into the kitchen. And when she got there the kindling-chips just flared up on the hearth, and round the flame there were Brownies dancing in a ring—all tiny little men no bigger than half an ell. They wore little fur coats; their caps and shoes were red as flames; their beards were grey as ashes, and their eyes sparkled like live coal.

More and more of them danced out of the flames, one for each chip. And as they appeared they laughed and chirped, turned somersaults on the hearth, twittered with glee, and then took hands and danced in a ring.

And how they danced! Round the hearth, in the ashes, under the cupboard, on the table, in the jug, on the chair! Round and round! Faster and faster! They chirped and they chattered, chased and romped all over the place. They scattered the salt; they spilt the barm; they upset the flour—all for sheer fun. The fire on the hearth blazed and shone, crackled and glowed; and the old woman gazed and gazed. She never regretted the salt nor the barm, but was glad of the jolly little folk whom God had sent to comfort her.

It seemed to the old woman as though she were growing young again. She laughed like a dove; she tripped like a girl; she took hands with the Brownies and danced. But all the time there was the load on her heart, and that was so heavy that the dance stopped at once.

"Little brothers," said the Mother to the Brownies, "can you not help me to get a sight of my daughter-in-law's tongue, so that when I can show my son what I have seen with my own eyes he will perhaps come to his senses?"

And the old woman told the Brownies all that had happened. The Brownies sat round the edge of the hearth, their little feet thrust under the grate, each wee mannikin beside his neighbour, and listened to the old woman, all wagging their heads in wonder. And as they wagged their heads, their red caps caught the glow of the fire, and you'd have thought there was nothing there but the fire burning on the hearth.

When the old woman had finished her story, one of the Brownies called out, and his name was Wee Tintilinkie:

"I will help you! I will go to the sunshiny land and bring you magpies' eggs. We will put them under the sitting hen, and when the magpies are hatched your daughter-in-law will betray herself. She will crave for little magpies like any ordinary forest snake, and so put out her tongue."

All the Brownies twittered with joy because Wee Tintilinkie had thought of something so clever. They were still at the height of their glee when in came the daughter-in-law from supper with a cake for herself.

She flew to the door in a rage to see who was chattering in the kitchen. But just as she opened the door, the door went bang! the flame leapt, up jumped the Brownies, gave one stamp all round the hearth with their tiny feet, rose

68

up above the flames, flew up to the roof,—the boards in the roof creaked a bit, and the Brownies were gone!

Only Wee Tintilinkie did not run away, but hid among the ashes.

When the flame leapt so unexpectedly and the door banged to, the daughter-in-law got a start, so that for sheer fright she plumped on the floor like a sack. The cake broke in her hand; her hair came down, combs and all; her eyes goggled, and she called out angrily:

"What was that, you old wretch?"

"The wind blew up the flame when the door opened," said the Mother, and kept her wits about her.

"And what is that among the ashes?" said the daughter-in-law again. For from the ashes peeped the red heel of Wee Tintilinkie's shoe.

"That is a live ember," said the Mother.

However, the daughter-in-law would not believe her, but, all dishevelled as she was, she got up and went over to see close to what was on the hearth. As she bent down with her face over the ashes Wee Tintilinkie quickly let out with his foot, so that his heel caught the daughter-in-law on the nose. The Woman screamed as if she were drowning in the sea; her face was all over soot, and her tumbled hair all smothered with ashes.

"What was that, you miserable old woman?" hissed the daughter-in-law.

"A chestnut bursting in the fire," answered the Mother; and Wee Tintilinkie in the ashes almost split with laughter.

While the daughter-in-law went out to wash, the Mother showed Wee Tintilinkie where the daughter-in-law had set the hen, so as to have little chickens for Christmas. That very night Wee Tintilinkie fetched magpies' eggs and put them under the hen instead of hens' eggs.

III

The daughter-in-law bade the Mother take good care of the hen and to tell her at once whenever the chickens were hatched. Because the daughter-in-law intended to invite the whole village to come and see that she had chickens at Christmas, when nobody else had any.

In due time the magpies were hatched. The Mother told her daughter-in-law that the chickens had come out, and the daughter-in-law invited the village. Gossips and neighbours came along, both great and small, and the old woman's son was there too. The Wife told her mother-in-law to fetch the nest and bring it into the passage.

The Mother brought in the nest, lifted off the hen, and behold, there was something chirping in the nest. The naked magpies scrambled out, and hop, hop, hopped all over the passage.

When the Snake-Woman so unexpectedly caught sight of *magpies*, she betrayed herself. Her serpent's nature craved its prey; she darted down the passage after the little magpies and shot out her thin quivering tongue at them as she used to do in the Forest.

Gossips and neighbours screamed and crossed themselves, and took their children home, because they realised that the woman was indeed a snake from the Forest.

But the Mother went up to her son full of joy.

"Take her back to where you brought her from, my son. Now you have seen with your own eyes what it is you are cherishing in your house;" and the Mother tried to embrace her son.

But the son was utterly infatuated, so that he only hardened himself the more against the village, and against his Mother, and against the evidence of his own eyes. He would not turn away the Snake-Woman, but cried out upon his Mother:

"Where did you get young magpies at this time of year, you old witch? Be off with you out of my house!"

Eh, but the poor Mother saw that there was no help for it. She wept and cried, and only begged her son not to turn her out of the house in broad day-light for all the village to see what manner of son she had reared.

So the son allowed his Mother to stay in the house until nightfall.

When evening came, the old Mother put some bread into her bag, and a few of those kindling-chips which the poor girl had given her, and then she went weeping and sobbing out of her son's house.

But as the Mother crossed the threshold, the fire went out on the hearth, and the crucifix fell from the wall. Son and daughter-in-law were left alone in the darkened cottage. And now the son felt that he had sinned greatly against his Mother, and he repented bitterly. But he did not dare to speak of it to his wife, because he was afraid. So he just said:

"Let's follow Mother and see her die of cold."

Up jumped the wicked daughter-in-law, overjoyed, and fetched their fur coats, and they dressed and followed the old woman from afar.

The poor Mother went sadly over the snow, by night, over the fields. She came to a wide stubble-field, and there she was so overcome by the cold that she could go no farther. So she took the kindling-wood out of her bag, scraped the snow aside, and fit a fire to warm herself by.

But lo! no sooner had the chips caught fire than the Brownies came out of them, just the same as on the household hearth!

They skipped out of the fire and all round in the snow, and the sparks flew about them in all directions into the night.

The poor old woman was so glad she could almost have cried for joy because they had not forsaken her on her way. And the Brownies crowded round her, laughed and whistled.

"Oh, dear Brownies," said the Mother, "I don't want to be amused just now; help me in my sore distress!"

Then she told the Brownies how her silly son had grown still more bitter against her since even he and all the village had come to know that his wife truly had a serpent's tongue:

"He has turned me away; help me if you can."

For a while the Brownies were silent, for a while their little shoes tapped the snow, and they did not know what to advise.

71

At last Wee Tintilinkie said:

"Let's go to Stribor, our master. He always knows what to do."

And at once Wee Tintilinkie shinned up a hawthorn-tree; he whistled on his fingers, and out of the dark and over the stubble-field there came trotting towards them a stag and twelve squirrels!

They set the old Mother on the stag, and the Brownies got on the twelve squirrels, and off they went to Stribor's Forest.

Away and into the night they rode. The stag had mighty antlers with many points, and at the end of each point there burned a little star. The stag gave light on the way, and at his heels sped the twelve squirrels, each squirrel with eyes that shone like two diamonds. They sped and they fled, and far behind them toiled the daughter-in-law and her husband, quite out of breath.

So they came to Stribor's Forest, and the stag carried the old woman through the forest.

Even in the dark the daughter-in-law knew that this was Stribor's Forest, where she had once before been enchanted for her sins. But she was so full of spite that she could not think of her new sins nor feel fear because of them, but triumphed all the more to herself and said: "Surely the simple old woman will perish in this Forest amid all the magic!" and she ran still faster after the stag.

But the stag carried the Mother before Stribor. Now Stribor was lord of that Forest. He dwelt in the heart of the Forest, in an oak so huge that there was room in it for seven golden castles, and a village all fenced about with silver. In front of the finest of the castles sat Stribor himself on a throne, arrayed in a cloak of scarlet.

"Help this old woman, who is being destroyed by her serpent daughter-in-law," said the Brownies to Stribor, after both they and the Mother had bowed low before him. And they told him the whole story. But the son and daughter-in-law crept up to the oak, and looked and listened through a wormhole to see what would happen.

When the Brownies had finished, Stribor said to the old woman:

"Fear nothing, Mother! Leave your daughter-in-law. Let her continue in her wickedness until it shall bring her again to the state from which she freed herself too soon. As for yourself, I can easily help you. Look at yonder village, fenced about with silver."

The Mother looked, and lo! it was her own native village, where she had lived when she was young, and in the village there was holiday and merry-making. Bells were ringing, fiddles playing, flags waving, and songs resounding.

"Cross the fence, clap your hands, and you will at once regain your youth. You will remain in your village to be young and blithe once more as you were fifty years ago," said Stribor.

At that the old woman was glad as never before in her life. She ran to the fence; already her hand was on the silver gate, when she suddenly bethought herself of something, and asked Stribor:

72

"And what will become of my son?"

"Don't talk foolishness, old woman!" replied Stribor. "How would you know about your son? He will remain in this present time, and you will go back to your youth. You will know nothing about any son!"

When the old woman heard that, she considered sadly. And then she turned slowly away from the gate, went back to Stribor, bowed low before him, and said:

"I thank you, kind lord, for all the favour you would show me. But I would rather abide in my misery and know that I have a son than that you should give me all the riches and happiness in the world and I forget my son."

As the Mother said this, the whole Forest rang again. There was an end to the magic in Stribor's Forest, because the Mother preferred her sorrows to all the joys of this world.

The entire Forest quaked, the earth fell in, and the huge oak, with its castles and its silver-fenced village, sank underground. Stribor and the Brownies vanished, the daughter-in-law gave a shriek, turned into a snake, wriggled away down a hole, and Mother and Son were left alone side by side in the middle of the Forest.

The son fell on his knees before his mother, kissed the hem of her garment and her sleeve, and then he lifted her up in his arms and carried her back to their home, which they happily reached by daybreak.

The son prayed God and his Mother to forgive him. God forgave him, and his Mother had never been angry with him.

Later on the young man married that poor but sweet girl who had brought the Brownies to their house. They are all three living happily together to this day, and Wee Tintilinkie loves to visit their hearth of a winter's evening.

Little Brother Primrose and Sister Lavender

THE stronghold of a wise and noble princess was attacked by her enemies. The princess could not gather together her large and faithful army quickly enough to defend her castle, but had to fly by night with her little prince in her arms.

So she fled all through the night, and at daybreak they reached the foot of grisly Mount Kitesh, which was on the border of the principality.

At that time there were no more dragons anywhere in the world, nor fairies, nor witches, nor any monsters. The Holy Cross and human reason had driven them forth. But in the fastnesses of Mount Kitesh the last of the Fiery Dragons had found a refuge, and seven Votaress Fairies attended upon him.

That is why Mount Kitesh was so grisly. But at the foot of the mountain lay a quiet valley. There dwelt the shepherdess Miloika in her little willow cabin, and tended her flock.

To that very valley came the princess at dawn with her baby, and when she saw Miloika sitting outside her cabin she went up to her and begged: "Hide me and the little prince in your cabin through the day. At nightfall I will continue my flight with the prince." Miloika made the fugitives welcome, gave them ewes' milk to drink, and hid them in her cabin.

As evening approached, the kind and noble princess said: "I must go on now with the prince. But will you take my Golden Girdle and the prince's little Gold Cross on a red ribbon? If our enemies should chance to find us they would know us by the Girdle and the Cross. Put these two things by and take good care of them in your little cabin. When my faithful captains have gathered together an army and driven out the enemy, I shall return to my castle and there you shall be my dear friend and companion."

"Your companion I cannot be, noble princess," said Miloika, "for I am not your equal either by birth or understanding. But I will take care of your Girdle and your Cross, because in time of real sorrow and trouble even the heart of a beggar can be companion to the heart of a king."

As she said this, Miloika received the Girdle and the Cross from the princess for safe keeping, and the princess took up the little prince and went out and away with him into the night, which was so dark that you could not tell grass from stone, nor field from sea.

II

Many years passed, but the princess did not return to her lands nor to her castle.

Her great army and her illustrious captains were so disloyal that they all immediately went over to her enemies. And so the enemy conquered the lands of the good and noble princess, and settled down in her castle.

No one knew or could discover what had become of the princess and the little prince. Most probably her escape on that dark night had ended by her falling into the sea, or over a precipice, or perishing in some other way with her baby.

But Miloika the shepherdess faithfully kept the Golden Girdle of the princess and the prince's little Gold Cross.

The smartest and wealthiest swains of the village came to ask Miloika to marry them, because the Golden Girdle and the little Gold Cross on the red ribbon were worth as much as ten villages. But Miloika would have none of them for her husband, saying: "You come because of the Golden Girdle and the little Cross; but they are not mine, and I must take better care of them than of my sheep or my cabin."

So said Miloika, and chose a penniless and gentle youth to be her husband, who cared nothing about the Girdle and Cross of Gold.

They lived in great poverty, and at times there was neither bread nor meal in the house, but they never thought of selling either Girdle or Cross.

Within a few years Miloika's husband fell ill and died; and not long afterwards a sore sickness came upon Miloika, and she knew that she too must die. So she called her two children, her little daughter Lavender and her still smaller son Primrose, and gave them each a keepsake. Round Lavender's waist she bound the Golden Girdle, and round Primrose's neck she hung the Gold Cross on the red ribbon. And Miloika said:

"Farewell, my children! You will be left alone in this world, and I have taught you but little craft or skill; but with God's help, what I have taught you will just suffice for your childish needs. Cleave to one another, and guard as a sacred trust what your mother gave into your keeping, and then I shall always remain with you." Thus spoke the mother, and died.

Lavender and Primrose were so little that they did not know how their mother had come by the Girdle and Cross, and still less did they understand the meaning of their mother's words. But they just sat side by side by their dead mother like two poor little orphans and waited to see what would become of them.

Presently the good folk of the village came along and said that Miloika would have to be buried next day.

III

But that was not the only thing that happened next day. For when the people came back from the funeral, they all went into the house to gossip, and only Lavender and Primrose remained outside, because they still fancied that their mother would yet somehow come back to them.

Suddenly a huge Eagle pounced down upon them from the sky, knocked Lavender down, caught her by the Girdle with his talons, and carried her off into the clouds.

The Eagle flew away with Lavender to his eyrie, high up on Mount Kitesh.

It did not hurt Lavender at all to fly along like that, hanging by her Gold Girdle. She was only sorry at being parted from her only brother, and kept on thinking: "Why didn't the Eagle take Primrose too!"

So they flew over Mount Kitesh, and there, all of a sudden, Lavender saw what neither she nor anyone else of the inhabitants of the valley had ever seen; for everyone avoided the grisly mountains, and of those who had happened to stray into them not one had ever returned. What Lavender saw was this: all the seven Votaress Fairies who waited upon the Fiery Dragon assembled together upon a rock. They called themselves *Votaresses* because they had vowed, as the last of the fairy kin, to take vengeance upon the human race.

The Fairies looked up, and there was the eagle carrying a little girl. Now the Fairies and the Eagles had made a bargain between them that each should bring his prey to that rock, and there hold a prizecourt upon the rock to settle what was to be done with the prey and who was to have it. And for that reason the rock was called *Share-spoil*.

So the Fairies called out to the Eagle:

"Ho, brother Klickoon! come and alight on Share-spoil!"

But luckily the bargain was no sounder than the parties to it.

The Eagle Klickoon had taken a fancy to Lavender, so he did not keep to the bargain, nor would he alight on Share-spoil, but carried Lavender on to his eyrie for his eaglets to play with.

But he had to fly right across the summit of the Mountain, because his eyrie was on the far side.

Now, on the top of the Mountain there was a lake, and in the lake there was an island, and on the island there was a little old chapel. Around the lake was a tiny meadow, and all round the meadow ran a furrow ploughed in days of old. Across this furrow neither the Dragon, nor the Fairies, nor any monster of the Mountain could pass. About the lake bloomed flowers, and spread their perfume; there doves took refuge, and nightingales, and all gentle creatures from the mountains.

Neither clouds nor mist hung over the holy furrow-surrounded Lake; but evermore the sun and moon in turn shed their light upon it.

As Klickoon flew over the Lake with Lavender, she caught sight of the chapel. And as she caught sight of the chapel, she remembered her mother; and as she remembered her mother, she pressed her hand to her heart; and as she pressed her hand to her heart, her mother's trust, the Golden Girdle, came undone upon Lavender.

The Girdle came undone; Lavender dropped from the Eagle's talons straight into the Lake, and the Girdle after her. Lavender caught hold of the Golden Girdle and stepped over the reeds, and the water-lilies, and the water-weeds, and the rushes to the island. There she sat down on a stone outside the chapel. But Klickoon flew on like a whirlwind in a rage, because he could not come near the Holy Lake.

Lavender was safe enough now, for nothing evil could reach her across the furrow. But what was the good of that, when the poor little child was all alone on the top of the grisly Mount Kitesh, and none could come to her, and she could not get away?

IV

Meantime the people who had buried Miloika noticed that the Eagle had carried off Lavender. At first they all burst out lamenting, but then one of them said:

"Good people, it is really as well that the Eagle carried off Lavender. It would have been hard to find someone in the village who could take charge of the *two* children. But for Primrose alone we shall easily find someone who will look after him."

"Yes, yes," the others all immediately agreed, "it is better so. We can easily look after Primrose."

They stood yet awhile outside the cabin gazing in the direction towards which the Eagle had disappeared with Lavender into the skies, and then they went back indoors to drink and to talk, repeating all the time:

"There's not one of us but will be glad to take Primrose."

So they said. But not one of them troubled so much about Primrose as to offer him a drink of water, although it was very hot. Now Primrose was thirsty and went in to ask for water. But he was so tiny that not one of those people could understand what he said. Primrose wanted someone to get him his little wooden mug; but not one of those people knew that Primrose's little wooden mug was behind the beam.

When Primrose saw all this, he looked round the room for a moment, and then the child thought: "This is no good to me. I am left all alone in the world." So he leaned over the pitcher that stood on the floor, drank as much water as he could, and then set out to see if he could find his little sister Lavender.

He went out of the house and set off towards the sun—the direction in which he had seen the Eagle fly away with Lavender.

V

The sun was setting beyond Mount Kitesh, and so Primrose, always looking at the sun, presently came to Mount Kitesh, too. There was no one beside Primrose to say to him: "Don't go up the Mountain, child! The Mountain is full of terrors." And so he went on, poor, foolish baby, and began to climb up the Mountain.

But Primrose did not know what fear was. His mother had kept him safe like a flower before the altar, so that no harm, not even the smallest, had ever befallen him; he had never been pricked by a thorn, nor scared by a harsh word.

And so no fear could enter Primrose's heart, no matter what his eyes beheld or his ears heard.

Meantime, Primrose had got well up into the Mountain and already reached the first rocks and crags.

And there, below Share-spoil, the Votaress Fairies were all assembled and still discussing how Klickoon had cheated them. Suddenly they saw a child coming towards them, climbing up the Mountain. The Votaresses were delighted; it would be easy to deal with such a little child!

As Primrose came nearer, the Votaresses went down to meet him. In less than no time they had surrounded him. Primrose only wondered when he suddenly saw so many ladies coming towards him, each with a great pair of wings! One of the Votaresses went close up to the child to take him by the hand.

Now Primrose was wearing the little Cross round his neck. When the Fairy saw the Cross, she screamed and started away from Primrose, for she could not touch him because of the Cross.

But the Fairies had no intention of letting the child off so easily. They hovered about him in a wide circle and conferred softly about what was to be done with him.

Little Primrose's heart was untroubled within him. The Fairies conferred, and their thoughts were so black that they came out in a cloud of black forest wasps buzzing round their heads. But Primrose just looked at them, and as he could see no harm in them, how was he to be frightened? On the contrary, the wings of one of the Votaresses took his fancy, flapping like that, and so he toddled up to her to see what she was really like.

"That will do nicely," thought the Votaress. "I cannot touch him, but I will entice him into the Wolf's Pit."

For near by there was a pit all covered over with boughs, so that you could not see it; and the bottom of the pit was full of horrible stakes and spikes. Whoever stepped on the boughs was bound to fall through and kill himself on the spikes.

So the Votaress Fairy enticed Primrose to the Wolf's Pit, always slipping away from him, and he always following to see what her wings really were. And so they came to the Pit. The Fairy flew over the Pit; but poor little misguided Primrose stepped on the boughs and fell down the hole.

The Votaresses shrieked for joy, and hurried up to see the child perish on the spikes.

But what do Fairies know about a baby!

Primrose was light as a chicken. Some of the boughs and branches fell down with him, the branches covered the spikes, and Primrose was so small and light that he came to rest upon the leaves as if they had been a bed.

When Primrose found himself lying down upon something soft, he thought: "I suppose I had better go to sleep!" So he tucked his little hand under his head and went sound asleep, never thinking that he was caught in a deep hole and could not get out.

Round him there were still many bare spikes, and the wicked Fairies were bending over the Pit. But Primrose slept peacefully and quietly, as though he were bedded on sweet basil. Primrose never moved. His mother had taught him: "When you are in your bed, darling, shut your little eyes and lie quite still, so as not to frighten your guardian angel."

So the Fairies stood round the Pit, and saw the baby falling asleep like a little duke in his golden crib. "That child is not so easy to deal with, after all," said the Votaresses. So they flew off to Share-spoil, and took counsel as to how they might kill him, since they could not touch him because of the little Cross.

They argued and argued, and at last one of the Votaresses had an idea. "We will raise a storm," said she; "we will cause a terrific rain. A torrent will pour down the Mountain, and the child will be drowned in the Pit."

"Whoo-ee, whoo-ee!" howled the Votaresses. They flapped their wings for joy, and at once rose up into the air and above the Mountain to roll up the clouds and raise a storm.

VI

Little Lavender was sitting on the top of the Mountain on her island in the Holy Lake. Round her fluttered lovely butterflies, even settling on her shoulders; and the grey dove guided her young to her lap to let her feed them with seeds. A wild raspberry-cane bent over Lavender, and Lavender ate the crimson fruit, and wanted for nothing.

But she was all alone, poor child! and sad at heart, because she believed she was parted for ever from Primrose, her only brother; and, moreover, she thought: "Did anyone, I wonder, remember to give him a drink or to put him to bed?"

In the midst of these sad thoughts Lavender looked up at the sky and saw a mist, black as night, rolling up round the Mountain. Over Lavender and over the holy furrow-surrounded Lake the sun shone brightly; but all around the mist was gathering and rising, inky clouds drifted and whirled, rose and fell like a pall of smoke, and every now and again fiery flashes darted from the gloom.

It was the Votaresses, flapping their great wings, who had piled up those black clouds upon the Mountain, and it was from their eyes that the fiery flashes shot across the darkness. And then suddenly it began to thunder most terribly within the clouds; heavy rain beat down all around upon the Mountain, and the Votaresses howled and darted to an fro through the thunder and the rain.

When Lavender saw that, she considered: "Over my head there is sunshine, and no harm can come to me. But perhaps there is someone abroad on the Mountain in need of help in this storm."

And although Lavender thought there was never a Christian soul on the Mountain, yet she did as her mother had taught her to do in a storm: she crossed herself and prayed. And as there was still a bell in the ruined chapel, Lavender took hold of the rope and began to toll the bell against the storm. Lavender did not know for whom she was praying or for whom she was tolling, but she tolled for a help to anyone who might be in distress.

When the bell on the island began to ring so unexpectedly, after having been silent for a hundred years, the Votaresses took fright up there in the clouds; they got worried and confused; they left off making a storm; they fled in terror in all directions, and hid under the rocks, under the crags, in hollow trees, or in the fern.

In a little while the Mountain was clear, and the sun shone on the Mountain, where there had been no sunshine for a hundred years.

The sun shone; the rain stopped suddenly. But for poor little Primrose the danger was not yet over.

That first great downpour had formed a big torrent in the Mountain, and the wild water was rushing fast towards the very Pit where Primrose was sleeping.

Primrose had heard neither the storm nor the thunder, and now he did not hear the torrent either as it came rushing and roaring with frightful swiftness towards him to drown him.

The water poured into the Pit, poured in, and in a moment it had overwhelmed the child.

It covered him, overwhelmed him in a moment. There was not a thing to be seen, neither Pit, nor spikes, nor Primrose, nothing but the wild water foaming down the Mountain.

But as the flood rushed into the pit, it eddied at the bottom, surged round and up and back upon itself, and then suddenly the water lifted up the boughs and branches, and little Primrose, too, upon the boughs. It lifted him up, clean out of the Pit, and carried him downhill on a bough.

The torrent was so strong that it carried away great stones and ancient oaks, rolling them along, and nothing could stop them, because they were heavy and stout, and the torrent very fierce.

But tiny Primrose on his bough floated lightly down the flood, as lightly as a white rose-bud, so that any bush could stop him.

And indeed, there was a bush in the way, and the bough with Primrose caught in its branches. Primrose woke up with a start, caught hold of the branch with his little hands, climbed up into the bush, and there he sat on the top of the bush, just like a little bird.

Above Primrose the sun shone clear and sweet; below Primrose foamed the dreadful water; and he sat in the bush in his little white shirt, and rubbed his eyes in wonder, because he could not make out what had happened and what had waked him up so suddenly.

By the time he had finished rubbing his eyes the water had all run away downhill; the torrent was gone. Primrose watched the mud squelching and writhing round the bush, and then Primrose climbed down, because he thought:

"I suppose I ought to go on now, since they have waked me up."

And so he went on up the hill. And he had slept so sweetly that he felt quite happy, and thought: "Now I shall find Lavender."

VII

No sooner had the bell stopped ringing than the Votaresses recovered their strength. They took courage and crept out of their hidie-holes. When they got out, lo! the sun was shining on the Mountain, and there is nothing in the world the wicked Fairies fear more than the sunlight. And as they could not wrap the whole Mountain in mist all in a hurry, each one quickly rolled herself up in a bit of fog, and off they flew to the Pit to make sure that Primrose was drowned.

But when they got there and looked into the Pit, the Pit was empty; Primrose was gone!

The Fairies cried aloud with vexation, and looked all over the Mountain to see whether the water had not dashed him against a stone. But as the Votaresses looked, why, this is what they saw: Primrose going blithely on his way; the sun was drying his little shirt for him on his back, and he was crooning away to himself as little children will.

"That child will escape us at this rate," sobbed one of the Votaresses. "The child is stronger than we are. Hadn't we better ask the Fiery Dragon to help us?"

"Don't disgrace yourselves, my sisters," said another Votaress. "Surely we can get the better of a feeble infant by ourselves."

So said the Fairy, but she did not know that Primrose in his simplicity was stronger than all the evil and all the cunning in Mount Kitesh.

"We will send the She-bear to kill the child for us," suggested a Votaress. "Dumb animals do not fear the Cross." And she flew off at once to the bears' den.

There lay the She-bear, a-playing with her cub.

"Run along, Bruineen, down that path. There is a child coming up the path. Wait for him and kill him, Bruineen dear," said the Votaress.

"I can't leave my cub," answered Bruineen.

"I'll amuse him for you," said the Votaress, and straightway began to play with the little bear.

Bruineen went away down the path, and there was Primrose already in sight.

The great She-bear rose up on her hind-legs, stretched out her front paws, and so went forwards towards Primrose to kill him.

The She-bear was terrible to see, but Primrose saw nothing terrible in her, and could only think:

"Here's somebody coming and offering me his hand, so I must give him mine."

So Primrose raised both his little hands and held them out to the She-bear, and went straight up to her, as though his mother had called him to her arms.

Well, another moment, and the dreadful She-bear would seize him. She had come up to him, and would have caught and killed him at once had he offered to run. But she saw that she had time to consider how she had best take hold of him. So she drew herself right up, looked at Primrose from the right and from the left, and now she was going to pounce.

But at that very moment the little bear cub in the den began to squeal. One of the black wasps that always buzzed round the Votaress's head had stung him. The cub howled lustily, because, although the Bruins are a spiteful folk themselves, they won't stand spite from anybody else. So the cub squealed at the top of his voice, and when Bruineen heard her baby crying she forgot about Primrose and the Mountain! Bruineen dropped on all-fours and trundled away like fury to her den.

The angry She-bear caught the Votaress by the hair with her great paw. They fought, they rolled, they tore at each other, and left Primrose in peace.

Primrose followed the She-bear and looked on for a bit while they fought and scuffled; he looked, and then he laughed aloud, silly baby! and went on up the Mountain, and never knew what a narrow escape he had had!

VIII

Once more the Votaresses assembled on Share-spoil to discuss what was to be done about Primrose. They saw that they were weaker than he.

Moreover, they were getting tired of flying to Share-spoil and back and conferring about Primrose, and so they were very angry.

"Well, we will poison the child. Neither spells nor cunning shall help him now," they resolved. And straightaway one of them took a wooden platter and hurried off to a certain meadow in the Mountain to gather poison berries.

But Primrose, never dreaming that anybody should be talking about him or worrying their brains about him, walked gaily over the Mountain, cooing softly to himself like a little dove.

Presently he came to the poison meadow. The path led through the middle of it. On one side of the path the meadow was covered with red berries and on the other side with black. Both were poisonous, and whoever ate of either the one or the other was sure to die.

But how was Primrose to know that there was such a thing as poison in the world, when he had never known any food but what his mother gave him?

Primrose was hungry, and he liked the look of the red berries in the meadow. But he saw someone over there in front of him on the red side picking berries and seemingly in a great hurry, for she never raised her head. It was the Votaress, and she was gathering red berries to poison Primrose.

"That is her side," thought Primrose, and went over to the black berries, because he had never been taught to take what belonged to another. So he sat down among the black berries and began to eat; and the Fairy wandered far away among the red berries and never noticed that Primrose had already come up and was eating black ones.

When Primrose had eaten enough he got up to go on. But, oh dear! a mist rose before his eyes; his head began to ache most dreadfully, and the earth seemed to rock beneath his feet.

That was because of the black poison.

Poor little Primrose! indeed you know neither spells nor cunning, and how are you going to save yourself from this new danger?

But Primrose struggled on all the same, because he thought it was nothing that a mist should rise before his eyes and the ground rock beneath his feet!

And so he came up with the Fairy where she was picking berries. The Votaress caught sight of Primrose, and at once she ran on to the path in front of him with her plateful of red berries. She laid down the platter before him and invited him by signs to eat.

The Votaress did not know that Primrose had already eaten of the black berries; and if she had known, she would never have offered him red ones, but would have let him die of the black poison.

Primrose did not care for any more berries, because his head ached cruelly; but his mother used to say to him: "Eat, darling, when I offer you something, and don't grieve your mother."

Now this was neither spell nor cunning what Primrose had been taught by his mother. But it was in a good hour that Primrose did as his mother had taught him.

He took the plate and ate of the red berries; and as he ate, the mist cleared before his eyes, his head and his heart stopped aching, and the ground no longer rocked beneath his feet.

The red poison killed the black in Primrose's veins. He merrily clapped his hands and went on his way as sound as a bell and as happy as a grig.

And now he could see the top of the Mountain ahead of him, and Primrose thought:

"This is the end of the world. There is nothing beyond the top. There I shall find Lavender."

IX

The Votaress would not believe her eyes; she stared after Primrose, and there was he toddling along and the dreadful poison doing him no harm!

She looked and she looked—and then she shrieked with rage. She could not imagine by what miracle Primrose had escaped. All she could see was that the child would slip through her hands and reach the Lake, for he was getting near the top.

The Votaress had no time to fly to Share-spoil and confer with her sisters. In time of real trouble people don't hold conferences. But she flew straight to her brother, the thunder-voiced bird Belleroo.

Belleroo's nest was in a little bog on the Mountain, close to the furrow which ran round the Holy Lake. As he was an ill-tempered bird, he too could not cross the furrow, but the evil Things of the Mountain had appointed his place here on the boundary, so that he might trouble the peace of the Lake with his booming.

"Kinsman, brother, Belleroo," the Votaress cried out to Belleroo, "there is a child coming up the path. Delay him here at the furrow with your booming, so that he may not escape me across the furrow to the Lake. I am going for the Fiery Dragon."

No sooner had the Votaress said this than she flew like an arrow down the Mountain to fetch the Fiery Dragon, who was lying asleep in a deep gully.

As for Belleroo, he was always all impatience to be told to boom, because he was horribly proud of his loud voice.

Dusk was beginning to fall. It was evening. Nearer and nearer to the furrow came Primrose. Beyond the furrow he could see the Lake, and the chapel looming white on the Lake.

"Here I am at the end of the world; I have only to cross that furrow," thought Primrose.

Suddenly the Mountain rang with the most awful noise, so that the branches swayed and the leaves trembled on the trees, and the rocks and cliffs re-echoed down to the deepest cavern. It was Belleroo roaring.

His boom was terrible. It would have scared the great Skanderbeg himself, for it would have reminded Skanderbeg of the boom of the Turkish guns.

But it did not in the least frighten the little innocent Primrose, who had never yet been shouted at in grief or anger.

Primrose heard something making such a noise that the very Mountain shook, and so he went up to see what great thing it might be. When he got there, lo! it was a bird no bigger than a hen!

The bird dipped its beak in a pool, then threw up its head and puffed out its throat like a pair of bellows, and boomed—heavens, it boomed so that Primrose's sleeves fluttered on him! This new wonder took Primrose's fancy so much that he sat down so as to see from near by how Belleroo boomed.

Primrose sat down just below the holy furrow beside Belleroo, and peered under his throat—because by now it was dark—the better to see how Belleroo puffed out his throat.

Had Primrose been wiser he would not have lingered there on the Mountain just below the furrow, where every evil Thing could hurt him, but he would have taken that one step across the furrow so as to be safe where the evil Things could not come.

But Primrose was just a little simpleton, and might easily have come to grief just there, within sight of safety.

Primrose was much amused by Belleroo.

He was amused; he was beguiled.

And while he was amusing himself in this fashion, the Fairy went and roused the Fiery Dragon where he slept in a deep gully.

She roused him and led him up the Mountain. On came the fearsome Fiery Dragon, spouting flame out of both nostrils and crushing firs and pine-trees as he went. There wasn't room enough for him, you see, in the forest and the Mountain.

Why don't you run, little Primrose? One jump across the furrow, and you will be safe and happy!

But Primrose did not think of running away. He went on sitting quite calmly below the furrow, and when he saw the flames from the Dragon flaring up in the darkness, he thought to himself: "What is making that pretty light on the Mountain?"

It was a cruel fire coming along to devour Primrose, and he, foolish baby! sat looking at it, all pleased and wondering: "What is making that pretty light on the Mountain?"

The Votaress caught sight of Primrose, and said to the Fiery Dragon: "There is the child. Fiery Dragon! Get your best fire ready!"

But the Dragon was panting with the stiff climb.

"Wait a moment, sister, while I get my breath," answered the Dragon.

So the Dragon took a deep breath, once, twice, three times!

But that is just where the Dragon made a mistake.

Because his mighty breath caused an equally great wind on the Mountain. The wind blew, and bowled Primrose over the furrow and right up to the Holy Lake!

The Votaress gave one shriek, threw herself down on the ground, rolled herself up in her black wings, and sobbed and cried like mad.

The angry Dragon snorted and puffed; he belched fire as from ten red-hot furnaces. But the flames could not cross the furrow; when they reached the furrow they just rose straight upwards as if they had come up against a marble wall.

Sparks and flame crackled and spurted and returned upon Mount Kitesh. Half the Mountain did the Dragon set on fire, but he lost little Primrose!

When the wind bowled Primrose over like that, Primrose only laughed at being carried away so fast. He laughed once; he laughed twice....

X

On the island in the Lake, beside the little chapel, sat Lavender.

It was evening, but Lavender could not go to sleep because of the hurly-burly in the Mountain. Lavender heard the Votaresses howling and shrieking and Bruineen growling. She heard the Dragon come snorting up from his lair, and saw him spout fire all over the Mountain.

And now she saw the blazing flames shooting upwards to the skies.

But then she heard something—good gracious! what was it she heard? A laugh, like a little silver bell. Lavender's heart throbbed within her.

The tiny voice laughed again.

Then Lavender could bear it no longer, but called from the Island:

"Who is that laughing in the Mountain?" asked Lavender gently, and all a-tremble at the thought of *who* might answer.

"Who is that calling me from the Island?" answered little Primrose.

And Lavender recognised Primrose's baby-talk.

"Primrose! my own only Brother!" cried Lavender, and stood up white in the moonlight.

"Lavender, little sister!" cried Primrose; and, light as a moth, he stepped over the reeds and the rushes and the water-weeds to the Island. They hugged and they kissed; they sat down side by side in the moonlight by the little chapel. A little did they talk, but they were not clever at making a long story. They clasped each other's little hands and went to sleep.

XI

That was how they began to live day after day on the Holy Lake. Primrose was quite happy and desired nothing better.

There was clear water in the Lake, and there were sweet raspberries. There were plenty of flowers and butterflies in the meadow, and fireflies and dew by night. Nightingales and doves nested in the trees.

Every evening Lavender would make Primrose a bed of leaves, and in the morning she bathed him in the Lake and tied up his little shoes. And Primrose thought: "What do we want with a wider world than this within the furrow?"

Primrose was well off; he was only a baby!

And Lavender was happy, but she was troubled about Primrose, how she should look after him and get him food. Because God has so ordered it that the young folk can never get food without the old folk having to think about it.

That is so all the world over, and couldn't be otherwise even on the Holy Lake.

So Lavender was worried. "To-morrow will be St. Peter's Day. Will the raspberries be over when St. Peter's is past? Will the water grow cold and the sun fail when autumn comes? How shall we get through the winter all alone? Will our cottage in the valley go to rack and ruin?"

So Lavender worried, and wherever there is worry, there temptation comes most easily.

One day she sat and mused: "Oh dear! what luck it would be if only we could get back to our cottage!" Just then she heard somebody calling from the Mountain. Lavender looked, and there in the wood on the far side of the furrow stood the youngest of the Votaresses.

She was prettier than the other Votaresses, and loved finery. She had noticed the Golden Girdle on Lavender, and now she wanted that Golden Girdle above anything else in the world.

"Little girl, sister, throw me your Girdle," called the fairy across the furrow.

"I can't do that, Fairy; I had that Girdle from my mother," answered Lavender.

"Little girl, sister, it wasn't your mother's Girdle; it belonged to the princess, and the princess has been dead long ago. Throw me the Girdle," said the Fairy, who remembered the princess.

"I can't, Fairy; the Girdle is from my mother," repeated Lavender.

"Little girl, sister, I will carry you and your brother down to the valley, and no harm shall come to you; throw me the Girdle," cried the Fairy once more.

This was a sad temptation for Lavender, who so longed to get away from the Mountain! But all the same she would not sacrifice her mother's keepsake to the greedy fairy, but answered:

"I cannot, Fairy; I had the Girdle from my mother."

The Fairy went away quite sadly, but next day she came back and began again:

"Throw me the Girdle, and I will take you down the Mountain."

"I cannot, Fairy; I had the Girdle from my mother," Lavender answered once more, but with a very heavy heart.

For seven days did the Fairy come, and for seven days she tempted Lavender. Temptation is worse than the sharpest care, and poor little Lavender pined away, so great was her wish to get down to the valley. Yet all the same she would not give up the Girdle.

For seven days did the Fairy call, and for seven days did Lavender answer her:

"I cannot, Fairy; the Girdle is from my mother."

And when she answered thus on the seventh day, the Fairy saw that there was no help for it.

The Fairy went down the Mountain; she sat down on the last, lowest stone, shook down her hair and cried bitterly, so great was her desire for the Golden Girdle of the princess.

XII

Meantime the good and noble princess was not dead, but had lived for many a year in a far country with her son, the prince.

The princess never told anybody how high-born a lady she was, and her son was too young at the time of their flight for him to remember.

And so in that country not a soul knew—not even the prince—that they came of royal blood. But how could anybody tell that she was a princess, when she had neither crown nor Golden Girdle? And though she was good, gentle, and noble, that did not prove that she was a princess.

The princess lived in the house of a worthy peasant, and there she span and wove for his household.

In this way she earned enough to keep herself and her son.

The boy had grown up into a tall and handsome youth of unusual strength and power, and the princess taught him nothing that was not good and right.

But one thing was bad. The prince had a very hasty and fierce temper. So the people called him *Rowfoot Relya*, because he was so rough and strong—and so poor withal.

One day Rowfoot Relya was mowing his master's meadow, and lay down at noon in the shade to rest. And a young squire came riding by, and called to Relya:

"Hi, young man! jump up and run back along the road and find me my silver spur; it fell off somewhere on the way."

When Relya heard that, his princely blood, his hot and hasty blood, was roused to evil within him because the other had disturbed him in his rest and would send him out to find his spur.

"Won't I, by heaven!" cried Relya, "and you can lie here and rest instead of me!" And with that he sprang at the young squire, pulled him off his horse, and flung him down in the shade, so that he lay there for dead.

But Rowfoot Relya, still furious, rushed home to his mother, and cried out upon her:

"Wretched mother! why was I born a rowfoot churl, for others to send me out to find their spurs for them in the dust?"

Relya's face was quite distorted with rage as he said this.

The mother looked at her son, and her heart grieved sorely. She saw that there would be no more peace for her and her son, because she would have to tell him what she had so far kept secret.

"You are not a rowfoot churl, my son," replied the princess, "but an unfortunate prince." And she told Relya all about herself and him.

Relya listened; his eyes blazed with a strange fire, and he clenched his hands in bitter anger. Then he asked:

"Is there nothing left, then, mother, of our lands?"

"Nothing, my son, save a little Cross on a red ribbon and a Golden Girdle," answered his mother.

When Relya heard that, he cried:

"I am going, mother, and I shall bring back that Cross and Girdle, wherever they may be! Threefold will the sight of them increase my princely strength!"

And then he asked:

"And where did you leave the Cross and the Girdle, mother? Did you leave them with the chief of your captains for him and your great army to guard?"

"No, my son," replied the princess, "and it is a good thing that I did not, for my captains and my great army went over to the enemy, and are now feasting and drinking with the enemy and wasting my lands."

"Did you perhaps leave them in the lowest room of your castle, in the seventh vault, under seven locks?"

"No, my son, and it is a good thing that I did not, because the enemy got into my castle, broke open and ransacked its secret chambers, searched its nine vaults, and fed his horses upon pearls out of my treasure hoards," replied the princess.

"But where did you leave the Golden Girdle and the Cross on the red ribbon?" asked Relya, with flashing eyes.

"I left them with a young shepherdess in a willow cabin, where there are neither locks nor strong boxes. Go, my son, perchance you will find them there still."

Relya would not believe that the Girdle and Cross might be safe in a willow cabin when the noble princess's pearls had not been safe even in the ninth vault under her castle.

But his princely blood, so proud and masterful, was roused yet more to evil in Relya's veins, and he roughly said to his mother:

"Farewell, then, mother! I shall find the Cross and Girdle wherever they may be, and it shall be no jesting matter for those who would refuse to let me have them! I shall bring you back your Girdle and Cross, by the princely blood in my veins."

As Prince Relya said this, he took the blade of the scythe, fitted it with a mighty hilt at the forge, and then hurried out into the world to find his heritage. The earth rang beneath his feet; his hair streamed in the wind, so swiftly did he stride; and his murderous blade shone in the sun as though it were plated with flame.

XIII

So Relya went on without stopping. He strode on by day, and by night he did not rest; both great and small got out of his way.

It is far to Mount Kitesh, but Relya had no difficulty in finding out the way, because Mount Kitesh was known throughout seven kingdoms for its terrors.

On St. John's Day Relya bade farewell to his mother, and on St. Peter's Day he reached the foot of the Mountain.

When he reached the foot of the Mountain, he inquired after the willow cabin, the shepherdess Miloika, and the Golden Girdle and Cross.

"There is the cabin in the valley. Miloika we buried the first Sunday after Easter, and her children have the Girdle and Cross. As for the children, the Fairies have carried them off to Mount Kitesh," replied the villagers.

Very wroth was Relya when he heard that the Girdle and Cross had been carried off to Mount Kitesh. He was so angry that he could not make up his mind which to do first—hasten up the Mountain or find out about the castle, since that was uppermost in his desires.

"And where is the princess's castle?" shouted Relya.

"Over there, a day's journey from here," answered the villagers.

"And how stands it with the castle?" asked Relya, and his hand played with his sword. "Tell me all you know about it!"

"None of us has been in the castle, because the lords of it are hard of heart. Round the castle they have placed mutes for guards and savage bloodhounds. We cannot force our way past the bloodhounds, and we do not know how to persuade the guards," answered the villagers. "And within the castle are fine lords, drinking red wine in the halls, playing upon silver lutes, and tossing golden balls to each other over a silken carpet. In the outer hall are two hundred workmen cutting hearts out of mother-o'-pearl for targets for the lords. And when the lords make a great feast, they load their guns with precious stones and shoot at the hearts of mother-o'-pearl."

When the villagers told him this, a mist swam before Relya's eyes, so furious was he when he heard how wantonly the treasure in his mother's vaults was being squandered.

For a while Relya hesitated, and then he cried:

"I am going up the Mountain to win the Cross and Girdle, and then I shall return to thee, O my castle."

Thus cried Relya; he made the sword sing through the air above his head, and then strode swiftly up into Mount Kitesh. There he found the great Dragon asleep in the deep gully. You see, the Dragon had tired himself out with belching so much fire at Primrose, and now he had gone fast asleep to gather fresh strength.

92

But Relya was all impatience to fight someone so as to cool his anger and to prove his strength. He was tired of seeing everybody, both great and small, get out of his way all the time, so now he rushed up to the Fiery Dragon to rouse and dare him to mortal combat.

Relya was a Doughty Hero, and the Fiery Dragon was a Terrible Monster, and so their combat must be sung in verse, beginning where Relya rushed up to the Dragon:

> Childe Relya smote the Dragon on the side
> With the flat blade, to rouse him from his sleep.
> The Beast looked up, raising his grisly head,
> Beheld the hero Relya standing by.
> Up leapt the Dragon, with a rending blow
> O'erturns the cliff and widens out the gap
> To make a fitting space wherein to fight!
> Anon unto the clouds he rears him up;
> Anon on Relya pounces from the clouds,
> And so with Relya joins in mortal fray.
> Now groans the earth and splits the solid rock.
> With tooth and flame the Dragon turns to bay,
> And thrusts at Relya with his fiery head.
> But Relya waits him with a ready sword,
> And meets the onslaught with a ready sword;
> And with his weapon beating down the flame
> Seeks for the sword an undefended spot,
> Where he may smite the Dragon on the head.
> Deep bites the brand—so mighty was the shock
> That brand and bone no more will come apart.
> From dawn till noontide did the battle rage,
> And weaker grew the Dragon all the while,
> With brooding on the shame that galled his heart,
> Because the babe, young Primrose, had escaped.
> And stronger grew Childe Relya all the while,
> For he did battle for his heritage.
> When at high noon the sun burned overhead,
> Childe Relya swung his gleaming brand aloft
> Towards the sun, and called on Heaven for aid.
> Down fell the sword betwixt the Dragon's eyes—
> Full swiftly fell, yet lightly struck the blade,
> Yet with such force, it cleft the Beast in twain.
> Into the hollow falls the Dragon, slain,
> And as stretched him in his dying spasm,
> The monstrous limbs block up the ancient chasm.

Thus did the doughty Relya overcome the Fiery Dragon. But his brave arms and shoulders ached terribly. So Relya said to himself: "I shall never get over the Mountain at this rate. I must consider what I had better do." And Relya went back to the foot of the Mountain, and there the hero sat down on a stone and considered how he was to get across the Mountain, and how he was to overcome the monsters, and where he might find Miloika's children and with them the Golden Girdle and Cross.

Relya was deep in thought, but all of a sudden he heard somebody weeping and sobbing near him. Relya turned, and there was a Fairy sitting on a stone, her hair all unbound, and crying her heart out.

"What ails you, pretty maiden? Why do you weep?" asked Relya.

"I weep, O hero, because I cannot get the Golden Girdle from the child on the Lake," answered the Fairy.

When Relya heard that he was overjoyed.

"Tell me, maiden, how can I get to that Lake?" asked Relya.

"And who may you be, unknown hero?" returned the Fairy.

"I am Prince Relya, and I seek a Golden Girdle and a Cross on a red ribbon," replied Relya.

When the Fairy heard that, she thought within her evil heart: "How lucky for me! Let Relya get the Girdle away from the Lake and on to the Mountain, and I will soon destroy Relya and keep the Girdle for myself."

So the cunning Fairy spoke these honeyed words to Relya:

"Let us go, noble Prince! I will guide you across the Mountain. No harm will come to you, and I will show you where the children are. Why should you not have what is yours by inheritance?"

Thus sweetly did the Fairy speak, but in her heart she thought otherwise. Relya, however, was mightily pleased, and at once agreed to go with the Fairy.

So they went across the Mountain. Neither Fairies nor monsters touched Relya, because he was being guided by the young Votaress Fairy.

On the way the Fairy advised Relya and tried to fill his heart with anger.

"You should but see, noble Prince, how insolent these children are! Not even to you will they give the Girdle. But you are a hero above all heroes, Relya, so do not let them put you to shame."

Relya laughed at the idea that two children should withstand him—*him* who had cleft in twain the Fiery Dragon!

The Fairy then went on to tell him how the children had come up into the Mountain, and how they did not know how to get away from it again.

In her joy at the prospect of getting the Girdle, the Fairy talked so much that her cunning deserted her, and she chattered to Relya and boasted to him of her knowledge.

"They are silly children, without any cunning. Yet if they knew what *we* know they would have escaped us already. There is a taper in the chapel and a censer. If they would start the fire that is not lit with hands, and then light the taper and censer, they could go with taper and censer across the whole Mountain as if it were a church. Paths would open before them and trees bow down as they passed. But for us this would be the worst thing possible, be-

94

cause all we Fairies and Goblins in Mount Kitesh would perish wherever the smoke from the taper and censer spread. But what do these silly, insolent children know?"

If the Votaress had not been so overjoyed, she would surely never have told Relya about the taper and censer, but would have kept the secret of the Votaresses.

So they came to the furrow, and there was the Holy Lake before them.

XIV

The Prince peered cautiously from behind a tree, and the Fairy pointed out the children to him. Relya saw the little chapel on the island. Before the chapel sat a little girl, pale as a white rose. She neither sang nor crooned, but sat still with her hands clasped in her lap and her eyes raised to heaven.

On the sand beside the chapel played a little boy, baby Primrose, and round his neck hung a little Gold Cross.

He played on the sand, built castles and pulled them down again with his tiny hands, and then laughed at his handiwork.

Relya watched, and as he watched he began to think. But the Votaress had no time to wait while the Prince finished thinking things out, so she softly prompted Relya.

"I will call to the little girl, noble Prince, and you shall see that she will not give up the Girdle; then do you draw your burnished sword, go up and take what is yours, and then come back to me to the Mountain, and I will guide you back down the Mountain so that my sisters shall not hurt you."

As the Fairy said this, she secretly rejoiced, thinking how easily she would kill Relya and get the Girdle for herself, so long as Relya would bring it from the Lake. But Relya only listened with half an ear to what the Votaress was saying, for he was lost in looking at the girl.

The Fairy called to Lavender:

"Little girl, sister, throw me the Girdle, and I will take you and your brother down the Mountain."

When Lavender heard this, her face grew yet paler, and she clasped her little hands yet more tightly. She was so sad that she could scarcely speak. She would so gladly have left the Mountain; her little heart was bursting with longing.

But all the same she would not part with her mother's Girdle.

Tears flowed down Lavender's face; she wept softly, but through her tears she answered:

"Go away, Fairy, and do not come back again, because you will not get the Girdle."

When Relya saw and heard this, his princely blood, his noble blood, was roused within him, but to a good purpose.

He was filled with pity for these two poor orphans in the midst of the grisly Mount Kitesh, defending themselves all alone against monsters and temptations, death and destruction. "Great Heavens!" thought he, "the princess trusted in her armed warriors and her strongholds to defend her lands, and the lands were lost; but these babes are left alone in the world, they have fallen among Fairies and Dragons, yet neither Fairies nor Dragons can rob them of what their mother gave them." All Relya's face changed as his heart went out with pity to the children. Thus changed, he turned towards the Votaress.

The Votaress looked at Relya. Why did he raise his sword? Was it to cut down those insolent children? No; Relya raised the sword aloft and threatened the wicked Fairy with it.

"Fairy, avaunt! as if you had never been! If you had not been my guide across the Mountain, I would strike your fair head from off your shoulders. I was not born a prince, nor did I forge this mighty sword that I might roam the world a spoiler of the fatherless!"

The poor Votaress was quite frightened. She started, and then fled to the hills. And Relya shouted after her:

"Go, Fairy! call your fairies and monsters! Prince Relya does not fear them!"

When the Fairy had run off to the hills, Relya crossed the furrow and went towards the children on the island.

How happy was Lavender when she saw a human being coming towards them and looking at them kindly! She sprang to her feet and stretched out both her arms, as a captive bird spreads its wings when you open your hand and let it go free.

Lavender was quite certain that Relya had come up only to bring them safe back from the Mountain. She ran to Primrose, took him by the hand, and both crossed over to Relya by the little bridge which they had fashioned with their own tiny hands across the reeds.

XV

A doughty hero was Relya, and he felt strange talking to children. But the children did not feel in the least strange talking to a hero, because they thought kindly of everybody, and there was no guile in their hearts.

Primrose took hold of Relya's hand and looked at his great sword. The sword was twice as big as Primrose! Primrose reached up with his little hand; he stood on tip-toe, and yet he could scarcely touch the hilt of it. Relya looked, and never had he seen such tiny hands beside his own. Relya was now in a sad quandary; he forgot all about the Girdle and Cross as he thought: "What shall I say to these poor orphan babes? They are little and foolish, and they do not understand."

Just then Lavender asked Relya:

96

"And how shall we get out of the mountains, my lord?"

"Well, that is quite a sensible little girl," considered Relya. "Here am I, marvelling how small and foolish they are, and never thinking that, after all, we have to get out of the mountains."

Then Relya remembered what the Votaress had told him about the taper and censer.

"Listen to me, little girl! The Votaress has gone to call her sisters to help her, and I am going on to the Mountain to meet them. Please God, I shall overcome the Votaress Fairies, return to you by the Holy Lake, and lead you away from the Mountain. But if the fairies should overcome me, if I perish on the Mountain, then do you start the fire that is not lit with hands, light the taper and censer, and you will pass over the Mountain as though it were a church."

When Lavender heard this, she was sadly grieved, and said to Prince Relya:

"You must not do that, my lord! What shall we poor orphans do if you perish on the Mountain? You have only just come to be our protector, and if you were to leave us straightway and get killed what should we do? Let us rather set to at once and start the fire, so as to light taper and censer, and do you, my lord, go forth with us over the Mountain."

But at that Relya became very angry, and said:

"Don't talk foolishness, you silly child! I was not born a hero for taper and censer to lead me while yet I wear sword by my side."

"Not taper and censer will lead you, but God's will and commandment," replied Lavender.

"Don't talk foolishness, you silly child! My sword would rust were I to be led by taper and censer."

"Your sword will not rust when you go a-mowing in field and meadow."

Relya was troubled. It was not so much Lavender's words as the sweet, serious look in the little girl's eyes that troubled him. He knew well enough that he would scarcely overcome the fairies and monsters, and that he would most probably perish if he were to go out to fight on the Mountain.

Little Primrose flung his arms round Relya's knees and looked at him coaxingly. And Relya's princely heart beat quick in his bosom, so that he forgot about Cross and Girdle and fight and castle, and all he could think was: "Well, I have to protect and save these faithful little orphans."

So he said:

"I will not throw away my life out of sheer wilfulness. Come, children, start the fire, light taper and censer; your little hands shall lead me."

XVI

A few moments later, and there was a wondrous marvel to be seen on Mount Kitesh.

A wide path opened all the way down the Mountain, and on the path grew turf as soft as silk. On the right-hand side walked little Primrose, still in his little white shirt, and in his hand he held an ancient wax taper, burning serenely and crackling softly, as though it were talking with the sun. On the left walked Lavender, wearing the Golden Girdle and swinging a silver censer, from which rose a cloud of white smoke. Between the two children strode Relya, tall and strong. It seemed strange to him, in his strength and valour, that taper and censer should thus guide him and not his own good sword. But he smiled gently at the children. His great sword hung over his shoulder, and as he strode on he said to the sword:

"Do not fear, my faithful friend. We shall go a-mowing in field and meadow; we shall clear scrub and forest; we shall hew rafters and build steadings. The sun will gild thee a thousand times while thou art winning bread for these two orphan babes."

So they went across the Mountain as though it were a church. A thin wraith of smoke rose from the taper, and sacred odours spread from the censer.

But woe and alas for the Votaresses on Mount Kitesh! wherever the smoke and the odour of incense spread upon the Mountain, there the Votaresses perished and died. They made an end, each one as it seemed most beautiful and fitting to her.

One turned herself into a grey stone, and then hurled herself down the rocks into a chasm, where the stone broke into a thousand splinters.

The second changed into a crimson flame, and then at once went out, puff! into the air.

The third dissolved into fine coloured dust, scattering herself over rock and fern. And so each of them chose what seemed to her the most beautiful way to die.

But it really didn't matter in the least. One way or another, they all had to leave this world, and even the most beautiful ways of dying could not make up for that!

In this way all the seven Votaress Fairies perished, and that is why there are no fairies, nor dragons, nor monsters now on Mount Kitesh or anywhere else in the world.

But Relya and the children reached the valley in safety, and Lavender took them to their cottage. And only then did Relya remember why he had gone up Mount Kitesh.

XVII

They went into the cottage and rested a little. Lavender, who knew where was her mother's modest store cupboard, brought out a little dry cheese, and they refreshed themselves.

But now Relya was puzzled what to do about those two orphans. Ever since they had come down into the valley, Relya's mind had begun to run once more upon the castle and upon his promise to his mother that he would bring her back the Cross and Girdle.

Therefore Relya said to Lavender:

"Listen to me, little girl: you will have to give me the Golden Girdle and Cross now, you and your brother, because they belong to me."

"But we belong to you too, my lord," said Lavender, and looked at Relya quite astonished, because he had not grasped that before.

Relya laughed, and then he said:

"But I must take the Girdle and Cross to my mother."

When Lavender heard that, she cried out overjoyed:

"Oh, sir, if you have a mother, do go and bring her here to us, because we have no mother now."

A stone would have wept to hear little Lavender speak of her mother in that poor and bare little cottage! A stone would have wept at the thought that so lovely a child should be left all alone in the world, when she turned to Prince Relya and begged him to bring them a mother because their mother was dead.

Again Relya was filled with pity, so that he almost wept. Therefore he bade the children good-bye and went away to fetch his mother.

XVIII

It took Relya seven days to return to his mother. She was waiting for him by the window, and when she saw him coming, lo, there was Relya coming home without sword, Cross, or Girdle. Relya never gave her time to ask questions, but called to her in a gentle voice:

"Make ready, mother, and come with me, that we may guard what is ours."

So they set out together. And on the way the Princess asked Relya whether he had found the Cross and the Girdle, whether he had raised an army and had reconquered their castle and lands?

"I found the Girdle and Cross, mother; but I raised no army, neither have I reconquered our lands. We shall do better without an army, mother, for you shall see what is left to us of our heritage," said Relya.

After seven days' travel they reached the cabin where Lavender and Primrose were waiting for them.

Oh, my dear! but there is great joy when kind hearts foregather! The princess hugged Lavender and Primrose; she kissed their cheeks, eyes, hands, and lips, and would scarcely let them go, so dear were they to her, those orphan children from her lost lands!

XIX

And so they lived together in the valley, although the little cabin was rather too small for them. But Relya had strong hands, and he built them a little house of stone. Their lives were uneventful, but there was a blessing upon them. Primrose tended the ewes and lambs, Lavender looked after the house and garden, the princess span and sewed, and Relya worked in the fields.

The people of the village got to know the wisdom of the princess and Relya's strength. Presently they remarked how well the Golden Girdle became the princess, and, although none of them had ever seen the princess before, they said:

"She must be our noble princess." And so they gave Relya and the princess a great piece of land in the valley, and begged Relya to be their leader in all things and the princess to be their counsellor.

God's blessing was with Relya's strength and the princess's wisdom. Their fields and meadows increased; other villages joined them; gardens and cottages sprang up in the villages.

Meantime the fine lords in the castle went on drinking and feasting as before. Now this had gone on far too long, and although the vaults and cellars of the castle had been the richest in seven kingdoms, yet after so many years of waste there began to be a lack of precious stones.

First of all the gems gave out in the treasure vaults, and then the mother-o'-pearl in the passages. Yet a little while, and there was no more bread for the servants, who had grown lazy. At last there was not even meat for the bloodhounds and guards. The faithless servants rebelled, the hounds ran away, and the guards left their posts.

But all this did not trouble the fine lords, because they had dulled their wits with drinking and feasting. But one fine day the wine gave out. *Then* they decided to hold a council! They met in the great hall and debated upon where they should get wine, because round about the castle all was desolate: the inhabitants had left, and the vines had run wild in the vineyards.

So the fine lords debated. But their vengeful and rebellious servants had cut through the rafters of the great hall, and when the lords were in the midst of their conference the roof fell in upon them. They were buried under the ruins of the great tower of the castle and all of them killed.

When the servants heard the tower crashing and falling, they too deserted the castle.

And so the castle was left without hounds, servants, or fine lords, ruinous and deserted, and dead.

Soon the news of this spread through the land, but not a soul troubled to go and see what had happened in the dead castle. From all sides they flocked together and went to the foot of Mount Kitesh to beg Relya to be their prince, because they had heard of his strength and courage and of the wisdom of the noble princess. Wherefore the people promised with their own hands to build them a new castle, all fair and stately.

Relya accepted the people's offer, because he rightly judged that God had given him such great strength and courage, and had delivered him from his hot and cruel temper, so that he might be of use to his country.

So Relya became a prince; and the princess, who was getting old by now, yet lived to see great happiness in her old age. And when the princess and Relya, with Lavender and Primrose, entered their new and stately castle for the first time, the village children scattered evergreens and sweet basil on their path, men and woman pressed round the princess, seized the hem of her robe and kissed it.

But the princess, radiant with joy, remembered that but for the loyalty of Lavender and Primrose none of this would ever have come to pass. She clasped the children to her breast and said:

"Happy the land whose treasure is not guarded by mighty armies or strong cities, but by the mothers and children in shepherds' cots. Such a land will never perish!"

* * * * *

Later on Prince Relya married Lavender, and never in the world was there a princess sweeter and more lovely than Princess Lavender.

Primrose grew up into a brave and handsome youth. He rode a fiery dapple grey, and he would often ride over Mount Kitesh, upon whose summit men were building a new chapel by the Holy Lake.

Notes

Interpretation of Names, etc.

THE original names in these Fairy Tales are either taken from Slav folklore or chosen or composed so as to convey a suitable meaning. In the English text the translator has therefore tried to render the significance of the original names in English in preference to reproducing the Slav names in English spelling.

How Quest Sought the Truth.

1. *Bjesomar* (Rampogusto). The name given by the old Slavs in some regions to the ruler of evil and malignant forces. Analysed, the name might be translated as Cherish-goblin, one who cares for hobgoblindom.
2. *Svarožić* (All-Rosy). The ancient Slavs pictured the sunshine in the form of a beautiful youth named *Svarožić*, All-rose.

The names of the grandfather and his three grandsons—Witting, Bluster, Careful and Quest—are as near as possible equivalents of the original names *Vjest, Ljutiša, Marun* and *Potjeh*.

Fisherman Plunk and his Wife.

1. *Zora-djevojka* (the Dawn-Maiden). To this day many old folk-tales of the Slavs tell of the Dawn-Maiden who sails the sea in the early morning in her boat of gold with a silver paddle and dwells in the Island of *Bujan*.
2. *The Sea King.* Slovenes and Slovaks alike tell of a mighty and wealthy Sea King who reigns in the depths of the sea.
3. *The Island of Bujan* (the Isle Bountiful). This is a wonderful island, so named for its abundance and fruitfulness and luxuriant vegetation. It was the ancient Slav's conception of Paradise. To this day the Russians mention it in refrains and spells against sickness, for a plentiful harvest, etc.
4. *The Stone Alatir* (Gold-a-Fire). Is mentioned in ancient Slav tales as "the white burning stone on Bujan," and may perhaps be taken to stand for the sun.
5. *Sea Maidens* (Mermaids). In Slovene and Croatian folk-tales, as with us, this term is applied to fabulous sea creatures, which are beautiful women to the waist, and from the waist downward shaped like a forked fish tail.
6. *The dumb speech.* The Jugoslavs popularly believe that animals converse with each other in a special "language," and that certain human beings can "speak" and understand this "language."

7. *The Monstrous Snake*, the *Bird with the Iron Beak*, the *Golden Bee*. Three monsters which, according to folk-tales, stir up the waves, raise tempests, and provoke thunderstorms round the Isle of Bujan, whence the storms spread throughout the world.

Palunko (Plunk) has no special significance, but the sound suggests a doleful, feckless sort of person.

Winpeace is a translation of Vlatko.

Reygoch.

1. *Legen* (*Ledjan*) (Frosten city). An ancient marvellous city which is mentioned in Croatian folk-songs and tradition. *Leden* means *frozen, icy*.

2. *Regoč, Regoc* (Reygoch). A huge simple giant of fairy kin. He is mentioned by the poet *Gjorgjić*, of Dubrovnik (Ragusa), in his *Marunko*.

The name *Kosjenka* is derived from *kose* (hair), and indicates the little fairy's flowing tresses.

Apart from being a simple fairy-tale, this story contains an allegorical element. *Reygoch*, the benevolent, simple-minded giant, is a character from *Marunko*, by the poet Gjorgjić, of Dubrovnik. The city of *Legen*, or *Ledjan* (which, to all intents and purposes, means "frozen"), is to be found in Croatian folk-tales and ballads.

Bridesman Sun and Bride Bridekins.

1. *Mokoš* (Muggish). A mighty force which, according to the beliefs of the ancient Slavs, ruled the earth, and especially in marshlands. She is mentioned in connection with the heavenly thunder god. *Perun*.

2. *Kolede* (translated by *Yuletide*) A winter festival celebrated at the end of December in honour of the sun, whose power once more begins to increase in those days.

3. *Krijes* (translated by *Beltane*). A festival in honour of the summer sun at the time of his greatest strength.

4. *Omaja, omaha*. Water which is flung from the mill-wheel. To this day peasants bathe children in this water so that evil may be turned away from them.

A *Ban* is a Warden of the Marches.

Neva means *bride*. *Nevičica* is the diminutive of *Neva*.

Stribor's Forest.

1. *Domaći* ("home sprites," from *dom*, house, home), Brownies. In all Slav nations this is the name given to the little domestic sprites which haunt the hearth. They are sometimes harmful and sometimes beneficent.

2. *Malik Tintilinić* (Wee Tintilinkie). Old popular name for one of the most lively of these *domaći*.

Little Brother Primrose and Sister Lavender.

1. *Kitež* (Mount Kitesh). The Russian author Merežkovski mentions the mysterious Kitež region, an uninhabited forest, and the Lake Svetlojar (which latter name might very well be transliterated by the *Holy Lake*), which used to be inhabited by all sorts of monsters.

2. *Vile Zatočnice* (Votaress Fairies). The term *Votaress snakes* (*zmije zatočnice*) is popularly applied to snakes which are supposed to have taken a vow in the autumn not to go to sleep for the winter without having killed somebody.

3 *Relya* (*Hrelja*). A Croatian ballad makes mention of a certain Hrelja as a better and stronger hero than even Kraljević Mark.

The names *Rutvica* and *Jaglenac* have simply been translated into *Lavender* and *Primrose*.

Bukač is derived from *buka*, noise. Hence *Belleroo*.

Medunkda, from *medved*, a bear (Bruineen).

The term *božjak* (applied to Relya), which suggests a powerful, poverty-stricken churl, the translator has sought to render by *rowfoot* (a rough fellow).

CPSIA information can be obtained
at www.ICGtesting.com
Printed in the USA
LVHW042338180723
752480LV00002B/525

9 781789 872750